MURDER IN BETHNAL SQUARE

Borgo Press Books by S. Fowler Wright

Arresting Delia: An Inspector Cleveland Classic Crime Novel
The Attic Murder: An Inspector Combridge & Mr. Jellipot Classic Crime Novel
The Bell Street Murders: An Inspector Combridge & Mr. Jellipot Classic Crime Novel
Beyond the Rim: A Lost Race Fantasy
Black Widow: A Classic Crime Novel
The Capone Caper: Mr. Jellipot vs. the King of Crime: A Classic Crime Novel
Crime & Co.: An Inspector Cleveland Classic Crime Novel
Dawn: A Novel of Global Warming
Dead by Saturday: An Inspector Cleveland Classic Crime Novel
Dream; or, The Simian Maid: A Fantasy of Prehistory (Marguerite Cranleigh #1)
Elfwin: An Historical Novel of Anglo-Saxon Times
The End of the Mildew Gang: An Inspector Cauldron Classic Crime Novel (Mildew Gang #3)
Four Callers in Razor Street: An Inspector Combridge & Mr. Jellipot Classic Crime Novel
The Hanging of Constance Hillier: An Inspector Cleveland Classic Crime Novel
The Hidden Tribe: A Lost Race Fantasy
The Jordans Murder: An Inspector Combridge & Mr. Jellipot Classic Crime Novel
The King Against Anne Bickerton: A Classic Crime Novel
The Mildew Gang: An Inspector Cauldron Classic Crime Novel (Mildew Gang #1)
Murder in Bethnal Square: An Inspector Combridge & Mr. Jellipot Classic Crime Novel
The Police and the Public: Some Thoughts on the British System of Justice
Post-Mortem Evidence: An Inspector Combridge & Mr. Jellipot Classic Crime Novel
The Return of the Mildew Gang: An Inspector Cauldron Classic Crime Novel (Mildew Gang #2)
The Rissole Mystery: An Inspector Combridge & Mr. Jellipot Classic Crime Novel
The Screaming Lake: A Lost Race Fantasy
The Secret of the Screen: An Inspector Combridge & Mr. Jellipot Classic Crime Novel
Spiders' War: A Novel of the Far Future (Marguerite Cranleigh #3)
Three Witnesses: A Classic Crime Novel
Too Much for Mr. Jellipot: An Inspector Combridge & Mr. Jellipot Classic Crime Novel
The Vengeance of Gwa: A Fantasy of Prehistory (Marguerite Cranleigh #2)
Was Murder Done? A Classic Crime Novel
Who Murdered Reynard? A Classic Crime Novel
The Wills of Jane Kanwhistle: An Inspector Combridge & Mr. Jellipot Classic Crime Novel
With Cause Enough?: An Inspector Combridge & Mr. Jellipot Classic Crime Novel

MURDER IN BETHNAL SQUARE

AN INSPECTOR COMBRIDGE AND MR. JELLIPOT CLASSIC CRIME NOVEL

by

S. FOWLER WRIGHT

WRITING AS "SYDNEY FOWLER"

THE BORGO PRESS

An Imprint of Wildside Press LLC

MMIX

CONTENTS

CHAPTER I.

MR. JELLIPOT AND AN IMPORTUNATE WIFE

MR. JELLIPOT looked at the woman who sat in tearful appeal at the side of his office desk. It was not his nature to be rude to women, nor indeed to men without much more cause than he had now, and the irritation he felt was only mildly evident in his voice as he said: "I am afraid, Mrs. Forbes, that it is not a case I can undertake. I am not accustomed, neither do I desire, to practise in the criminal courts. There are firms—I can recommend you to one, if you desire—who specialise in defending those who are accused of capital crimes, and who would be far more competent than I can profess to be."

Alice Forbes was not naturally an aggressive woman, but he was fighting for the life of one whom she had the good or bad fortune to love, and it gave spirit to her reply: "You don't really mean that?"

Mr. Jellipot, from being mildly irritated, became mildly surprised. He was habitually exact of speech, and was seldom, if ever, accused of saying that which he did not mean. He was naturally diffident of his own powers, and it was a fact that the notorious murder cases in which he had been engaged had been forced upon, rather than sought, by him. But he did honestly think that, if he should undertake the defence of this woman's probably most objectionable and homicidal husband, the man would be represented less competently than by Jones & Littlepin, or Crompton Moss. He avoided a point on which his conscience was less than sure.

"Will you tell me why you have come to me?" he asked, and her heart leapt as she heard the words, with a swift instinctive consciousness that he temporised, and would be certain to yield at last.

"I came to you," she said, "because it's so similar to the murder in Razor Street[1]—I mean the puzzle's almost exactly the same—and you got Miss Barman off when everyone thought she'd be convicted for certain sure. I know when I read the papers I thought she'd done it myself, though I didn't think he was much loss, and I don't suppose anyone did."

Mr. Jellipot remembered that she *had* done it, which was something he could not say, but it disinclined him more than before to be drawn into such a battle again. Alice Forbes saw that she had said the wrong thing, though she could not understand where her error lay. She added: "I suppose you think it was a cheek walking into your office without any introduction or anything. But when you are in such trouble as mine—! And I don't want you to think that I can't pay."

She opened a shabby handbag, from which she took a little roll of bank notes, sixty pounds in all, which she had brought to satisfy, if it would, the traditional rapacity of the law.

Mr. Jellipot looked at them with distaste. In his commercial practice he would charge with a liberal, even at times a high conception of the value of what he did. But that was a different matter. There, large sums of money would be at stake, to be lost or won: contracts would be signed by which commercial enterprises were launched or sold, and much would hang upon the expertness and accuracy with which they were drawn. He took money where money was being wagered or made. He had no compunction in that.

But these criminal charges must be contested at a cost which could not be recovered even by an innocent man, often with money representing years of penurious thrift, which would be swept in an hour, like chicken feed, into some wealthy barrister's bulging purse! His distaste for its financial aspects was not the least of the causes which disinclined him to cultivate business which had come of late with increasing frequency to his door.

"You had better put that back," he said, with more geniality in his tone than she had heard previously, "till you are asked. You'll find that will happen quite soon enough. What I meant was that, if your husband's trouble is at all like that in which Miss Barman found herself, it doesn't follow that I should be the one who would be most likely to get him out. The mere fact that I was instructed might prejudice the jury, as soon as they heard my name. And besides, things don't go the same way twice. And I think I should tell

---

[1] See *Four Callers in Razor Street.*

you, Mrs. Forbes, that Miss Barman didn't get off through anything that I was able to do. The case developed quite unexpectedly."

Mrs. Forbes appeared to be unimpressed by these warnings. "I don't mind how unexpected it is," she said stubbornly, "so that it ends in the right way."

Mr. Jellipot had a disposition to ask her how recently she had read the parable of the importunate widow, whom she understudied so well. She was not a widow. But she might be one in three months, or even a little less, if her husband were to be hanged for a crime of which he was most probably guilty. Still, it wouldn't do to say that! He checked an errant thought to ask: "Before I can discuss this further, I must put a question to you, to which, in your husband's interest, I must urge you to give an absolutely frank reply, and which I shall treat as absolutely confidential under whatever circumstances: Are you really sure that your husband is an innocent man?"

"Yes," she said with an obvious, if inconclusive, sincerity, "there's no doubt about that."

"But you have reason to think that the police may not agree?"

"Inspector Combridge thinks he did it. You could tell that from the way he talked."

"I have found Inspector Combridge to be very shrewd, and he is certainly a fair-minded man. Why should he think that, if it is not true?"

"Because of what Basil wrote, and him being there."

"Perhaps," Mr. Jellipot said, with a sigh for his own weakness, for he saw his feet slip on the edge of a pit he would have preferred to miss, "you'd better tell me the whole tale?"

9

CHAPTER II.

Murder in Bethnal Square

MRS. FORBES did not object, but it appeared that, on this subject at least, she lacked a fluent narrative style. She seemed to find it hard to begin, and Mr. Jellipot watched her silently, offering no help. She said at last: "It was about some silly letters I wrote three years ago."

"Before you were married to Mr. Forbes?"

"Yes, of course."

"Letters to the murdered man?"

"Yes. To Mr. Coldwater."

"If they were written before your marriage, you need not have been greatly concerned?"

Mrs. Forbes did not appear to agree. "They were silly letters," she repeated. "Very silly. Not the sort you want anyone else to read."

"You didn't wish Mr. Forbes to see them. Did you think it would make serious trouble?"

"No. Not serious. Not what you'd call serious. It—it would have been worse than that."

"I'm afraid I don't understand."

"I mean Basil would have laughed. It wouldn't have been a thing he'd ever forget."

Mr. Jellipot said "Yes. I see," as in fact he did. He had not practised for over thirty years without learning something of the incomprehensible folly of girls when a pen is in their hands and a man in their thoughts; and he knew something of the use to which such letters are often put when in unscrupulous hands. He knew, also, that it is not, in most instances, as is popularly supposed, the fear of tragic quarrel which renders their writers desperate in later years to prevent them coming to the sight of husbands, lovers, or children. It is the fear—perhaps the certainty—of ridicule, of exposure of a weakness

10

which may be absurdly inconsistent with the assumed or attributed character of discreeter years. Alice Forbes had been something to her husband which the sight of those letters would have destroyed for ever. And he would not have taken it in a tragic mood. Worse than that. Basil would have laughed. Yes, Mr. Jellipot had no doubt that he understood.

But it seemed that, if he were to have this tale fully told, it would only be in reply to questions from him. He asked: "And where are those letters now?"

"I burned them yesterday. Before I heard what had happened."

Mr. Jellipot was puzzled. He had supposed that Basil Forbes was suspected of murdering Mr. Coldwater in a chivalrous attempt to recover them on his wife's behalf, but it seemed that the tale was to be less simple than that. He wished that the woman had the will or the wit to tell it in a straightforward manner, but, as he could not have it in his own way, it must be in hers. He asked: "How had you got them back?"

"Mr. Coldwater promised them to me when I'd paid him a hundred pounds. I'd paid fifty-four, and I had a legacy which was enough to settle the balance and a bit more. So I went to see him, and bought them back."

"When was that?"

"Yesterday morning."

"The day Henry Coldwater was killed?"

"Yes. Just before. I mean a few hours before."

"And your husband knew about this?"

"He didn't know the legacy, or that I was getting them back. He knew about the pound a week."

"You mean that you had been paying the hundred pounds at the rate of a pound a week? If your husband knew that, there wasn't much more for him to know, was there?"

"I didn't know that he'd found that out."

"So I suppose he went to get the letters after they had been returned to you?"

"Yes."

"And what—what does he say—happened then?"

"He thought Henry was telling lies. He says he thrashed him, and he still kept saying the same, as of course he couldn't help doing, so Basil said at last he'd ask me if it were true, and if it wasn't he'd go back and thrash him again."

"And he may have thrashed him rather too hard?"

11

"No, he didn't do anything silly like that. He says Henry was all right when he came away. It was after that someone went and stuck a bayonet into him out of the grate."

"A bayonet?"

"Yes. Henry's father'd brought it back from the war. He used to keep it in the fender to break the coal."

"Well," Mr. Jellipot said, "anybody could have picked it up. It isn't as though he'd been killed with something your husband took into the room."

"Of course not," she agreed eagerly. "You'd think anyone would see that."

"But," he went on, not wishing to encourage her too far in what might prove to be a vain hope, "it is also true that it would be most likely to be used by someone who had entered the room without any homicidal purpose, and who therefore had no lethal weapon in his possession. That is to say, it was one which might be snatched up, either with murderous purpose, or in self-defence, in the course of a quarrel that developed in Mr. Coldwater's room, as you say that that with your husband did."

Mrs. Forbes gave the solicitor an angry, almost suspicious stare, as the force of this argument penetrated her mind. "I suppose," she said, "you might make almost anything out, if you go guessing round. But I don't see that it's any use to us, saying that."

Mr. Jellipot sighed slightly, wondering why so many women have been created without the faculty of logical reasoning. Perhaps, he reflected, it may assist the directness of their approach. To see both sides with equal clarity may be a source of weakness rather than strength. He said aloud: "No. It probably isn't. But you said, if I understood you correctly, that your husband had written something of an unfortunate character?"

"Well, he had to write, because Mr. Coldwater wouldn't ever see anyone unless they made an appointment first, and said what their business would be. I don't think he liked meeting people unexpectedly, and besides, it made them understand how important he was. So there's nothing really in that."

"I should suppose the fact that your husband wrote to be in his favour rather than now. It shows that there was no concealment about his call. Unless, of course, there was something in the letter threatening Mr. Coldwater's life?"

"No, I'm sure there wouldn't be that."

"Perhaps you don't really know what it did say?"

"I haven't seen it. But it was something about breaking every bone in his body that Inspector Combridge seemed to think shouldn't have been there."

"And you don't think that should be taken seriously?"

"Not from Basil. It would be just what he would be likely to do."

Mr. Jellipot allowed himself to look slightly surprised. "You mean that he would be likely to break every bone in the body of a man with whom he might have a difference to adjust?"

"That's a way of speaking, of course. It only means that he'd give him a thrashing if he thought that it was the best thing for him to have and that was just what he did."

"Yes...it is a sound point. The threat is evidently not one to be taken literally. Nor, in fact, did it occur. I suppose your husband admitted having thrashed Mr. Coldwater, when he was questioned by the police?"

"Yes, of course. He's not the sort that tells lies. He said he was sorry when he came away that he hadn't given him more than he did. But when he found that I'd really had the letters, he thought it might have been about right, except for him having got hold of the hundred pounds."

Mr. Jellipot considered this with a mind disposed to be favourably influenced by Mrs. Forbes's confident belief in her husband's veracity. But he reflected that even a habitually truthful man, as he was willing to suppose Basil Forbes to be, might hesitate to accuse himself of a capital crime. And Inspector Combridge, if the woman were to be believed, was not favourably impressed. "Your husband," he asked, "has not, as far as you are aware, been arrested yet?"

"No. I thought, if I came to you at once, you'd stop anything happening like that."

"I am afraid you attribute more power to me than I possess. Where is Mr. Forbes now?"

"He's at the bank, of course."

"He's a bank employee?"

"He's the accountant at the New Oxford Street Branch of the London & Northern Bank."

"I suppose he knew you were coming to see me this morning?"

"Oh, no, he didn't! He told me not to put my foot into it at all. I expect he'll punish me when he does."

"Punish you?" Mr. Jellipot asked, mildly surprised again by the expression, and the cheerfulness with which it was mentioned. "Not seriously, may I hope?"

13

"He always beats me when I don't do what I'm told. I expect it's the best way."

"Mr. Forbes appears to be somewhat addicted to demonstrations of physical vigour. But such—may I say evidences of affection?—are not sufficiently serious to prevent you following your own judgment when it differs from his?"

"You see," she answered complacently, "he's a very strong man. I couldn't let him go to prison, if you mean that."

"We will hope," Mr. Jellipot replied, but without much confidence in his voice, "that the question does not arise. Mrs. Forbes, I am sorry that, at this stage, and on my present information, I cannot undertake to act for your husband, nor should I be disposed to do so if I had his instructions, which I have no reason to suppose that I ever shall. But if you will trust my discretion as to what use, if any, I may make of the information you have given me this morning, I will have a few words with the police, and may possibly be able—but I don't want you to hope too much—to relieve your mind of the fear which you how have.

"You must understand that it is the duty of the police to question—and perhaps to suspect—all who are on the scene of a crime of violence of this character. But they don't usually make an arrest without having very good reason for what they do. If you like to come to see me tomorrow morning, you may find me better able to advise you than I am now. At the present moment I have an overdue appointment of some importance with certain gentlemen who are almost certainly waiting with impatience in the outer office."

With these words the solicitor shook hands with Mrs. Forbes, and gently but firmly conducted her to the door.

CHAPTER III.

MR. JELLIPOT ENQUIRES

"IS that you, Combridge? Yes, Jellipot speaking. If I am not misinformed, you are interesting yourself in the decease of a Mr. Henry Coldwater, which took place in Bethnal Square yesterday afternoon?"

"Decease? Murder's the word. Yes, I certainly am. If you've got a good tip for me—"

"No. I am afraid I am seeking rather than offering information. But may I conclude from that remark that the case is not as simple as you would like it to be?"

"Well, there aren't many that are. Not on the first day. What is it you want to know?"

"What sort of a man was he?"

"He was a red-hot rogue. Whoever stuck him did the world a good turn. But it's rough on us. We've been trying to catch him for seven years, and we'd just baited a trap that would have had him doing one of the longest stretches the law allows."

"Do I understand that you regard it as a reflection upon the C.I.D. that he should have died without learning what a dock is like from an inside view?"

"Yes. That's what I was trying to say."

"What was his particular line of iniquity?"

"Oh, you might call him a general practitioner. Any kind of financial fraud. Been a solicitor's clerk, and learned all the law he could to put it to the wrong use. Selling businesses for ten times what they were worth was his special line. Used to write very clever letters to his victims, rather discouraging them from buying, and then talk to them just differently enough to pull them in. But he had other lines besides that. Blackmailing must have brought him in a good sum."

"So I have been led to infer. The fact is that I had a Mrs. Forbes in to see me this morning. She seemed to think—quite erroneously I expect—that the police were about to exhibit their usual ineptitude by arresting her husband for something he hasn't done."

"So he's getting the wind up, is he? That's always worth knowing. And I suppose I'm to have the pleasure of having you against me again?"

The inspector's tone suggested that it was a pleasure he would not object to miss, but Mr. Jellipot answered equably, taking the points which had been raised in his usual orderly manner.

"I don't think he's getting the wind up at all. I gathered that the lady came to see me without her husband's knowledge, and is anticipating a certain amount of marital difference—or perhaps discipline would be the more accurate word—if he should learn what she has done. But as I naturally declined to take instructions from her, and it is improbable that I should consent to act for Mr. Forbes even if he should ask me himself, the question of being against you does not arise, even if you had been contemplating his arrest, which I shall be pleased to assure the lady is not the case."

"I shouldn't go quite that far, if I were you. Anyway, you haven't had it from me."

"But I think I have. From what I have understood already, the case against Basil Forbes can only be strong in the absence of any alternative probability. I suppose that it would have influenced you—perhaps decisively—against him had it been a fact that he had come to me in anticipation of being arrested, but in the absence of that indication, if you have not already decided that you can find the criminal without looking further than him, I incline to think that it is very unlikely that you will do so at a later day."

"Well, have it your own way! But it isn't quite as simple as that. As a matter of fact, I should be glad to feel we could rule Forbes definitely out, because we should know what we're up against better than we do now. But he's not one who makes it easy to give him a clean ticket. The way he said that he hadn't killed Coldwater made it sound about level odds that he'd murder me. All the same, if you've got anything out of his wife that you're free to tell, and that you think it might be useful to me to know, I'll come round in the morning, and lap it up."

"I haven't much. But you can come round now if you like. I shan't have much leisure tomorrow."

"If you're sure that it's not too late?"

"No. I should have rung you up earlier in the afternoon, but I've had a full day. If you come now, I can give you any time up to an hour."

Inspector Combridge replied that he would be at Mr. Jellipot's Basinghall Street office as rapidly as the traffic lights would allow, and the solicitor telephoned to his housekeeper to say that he would be half an hour late for dinner, and received no more than a respectful "Yes, sir," in response, which, had they heard it, might have been the envy of a large number of married men.

Having settled that, he proceeded to the signing of letters, and the customary clearing of his desk from the litter which had accumulated during the day, so that when Inspector Combridge was announced he was able to listen with the free mind of one whose work, for that day, was done.

"You will appreciate...," he began, when the inspector was seated comfortably, and had succumbed to the temptation of one of the choice cigars which Mr. Jellipot kept for his most valued clients and friends, while limiting himself to one daily after-dinner indulgence—"you will appreciate that, though I am not acting professionally for Mr. Forbes, and though I received permission from his wife to use the information she gave me entirely at my own discretion, yet the obligation of confidence—the obligation to exercise that discretion in the interests of these two people—must still remain. I do not say that that consideration will restrain me from repeating freely what she has said to me—it may actually operate in an opposite direction—but I suggest that you should first tell me as much as you feel free to do concerning the circumstances of the crime, so that I may be better able to judge of what the position, as between Forbes and the law, is likely to be."

"Yes. I'll do that. There's nothing to keep back, as between you and me. But how much do you know now? I suppose you've read what's been in the press?"

"No. I can't say that I have. Not much more than the headlines. I've been too busy."

"Well, it's not a long tale. I've told you the kind of man Coldwater was. He was a queer fish. I don't mean that there's anything queer about being a rogue, but he had some queer ways, though I don't say that there may not have been some method in them.

"For one thing, he carried on his different businesses at Coldwater House—"

"Do you mean that his place of business had the same name as himself? That it was named after him?"

"No. It was the other way round. It's been Coldwater House for about sixty years, and he was a younger man. He either took the place because it had the same name as himself, and he thought it would sound well, or he changed his name, for the same reason, to match the property. But which it was, we've never been able to find out. When he attracted our notice first he was Henry Coldwater of Coldwater House, Bethnal Square, and we've never been able to get behind that."

"Well, it doesn't matter. You were going to say something about his different businesses?"

"Yes. That he carried them on separately on different days. He had employees who only came certain days of the week, so that some of them seem never to have met, though they've been on the staff for years; and he had one day—Monday it was—when he would be quite alone. On that day, his rule was that he would see people by appointment only, though it was one, as what happened yesterday shows, which wasn't always strictly observed.

"His own office was on the first floor, and he had a pull there that would release the catch of an inner door in the hall. Anyone calling to see him would have to ring first, and then he would call down a speaking tube, and if he expected them, or they were anyone he wanted to see, he would release the catch and tell them to come up, and to be very careful to close the door. But, in fact, it works on a spring, and if anyone pushes it open widely enough to pass through, it will close itself. The care wouldn't be needed to shut it, but to close it gently enough for it not to latch again.

"When I add that he kept records of the appointments he made, and that the list for Monday was on his desk when he was found, you'll understand that, unless someone called whom he hadn't expected, but whom he invited up when he heard who it was, we've got to pick from a small list."

"Yes. I see that. I see also why Mrs. Forbes described it as being a good deal like the Razor Street murder. But I shouldn't suppose that you'd have quite the same kind of difficulty that puzzled us then. The caller in this case wouldn't be likely to want to lift suspicion from others, hut only to save himself. Considering that those who called after Coldwater was dead would get no reply, and, I suppose, conclude sooner or later that he was out, and go away, you ought to be able to get very close to the right man. But you'll tell me that there's something that makes it less simple than that?"

"Well, I don't know. At present there's one man that we haven't found, and we don't know whether he'll say that he saw Coldwater alive, or couldn't make anyone hear. But, apart from that, there are one or two rather puzzling features. Not pointing in any particular direction, but just being unlikely things that give you the uncomfortable feeling that there's something about it that won't be easy to fit together."

"I think I've heard you say," Mr. Jellipot replied, "that the points that seem queerest at first are usually those that prove most useful in solving a difficult problem, which struck me as a very likely eventuality."

"Did I say that? Well, we'll hope it'll be true here. I expect you read that it's practically certain that the man was killed with a bayonet he used to keep in the grate?"

"It was told to me as a fact. 'Practically certain' is, I believe, an expression which usually means highly probable, but not certain at all. How does the measure of doubt arise?"

"The bayonet, if it were used, had been wiped clean, and put back in its place, and it bore no fingerprints. The first reason we had, in spite of that, for thinking it had been used was that there was no other weapon about, and that the blade exactly fits, not only the wound, but the holes in the clothes of the murdered man through which it was driven. It shows how firmly it was thrust in, and pulled out again—probably not immediately after—that these holes are so exact—I mean that there are no slittings at all. You might think that I put it too high when I say it's practically certain that it was used; but we've had a curious piece of evidence which increases the probability, and explains how it was cleaned.

"There's an elderly man named Cooper who occupies a third-story flat at 7, Bilton Crescent, and his back room overlooks the yard of Coldwater House, though it isn't a very near view.

"He says that he was alone on Monday afternoon, amusing himself with a bagatelle board, which seems to be a very frequent occupation with him. When he scores fifty or over (I don't know much about the game myself, but he assures me that, on his board, it isn't easy to do), he treats himself to a drink, and when he does that he usually stands at the window, and looks out over the back gardens of Bilton Crescent and Bethnal Square.

"He says that on that Monday afternoon he scored over fifty three times, and on one of those occasions (but unfortunately he can't remember which, or what time it was, not thinking it to have been of any importance at the time), he saw a man come out of the back door of Coldwater House, and go to a tap in the yard, and very carefully wash what looked like a long knife; and may well have been this bayonet, with which the murder had been committed a few minutes before."

"He might have been seen by any of some scores of other people?"

"Yes. But we can't find that he was."

"It sounds to me," Mr. Jellipot said deliberately, "an incredible tale."

"So it did to us. But Cooper seems to be a respectable and intelligent man, and there is no apparent reason why he should lie. Besides that, it is consistent with—indeed, it explains—the condition in which the bayonet was left."

"Does Cooper say that he could recognise the man if he should see him again?"

"No. He says definitely that he couldn't. The most we can get is that he was wearing a dark overcoat and a bowler hat, and that he wasn't a particularly large man. And the last point, if it be reliable, lets Forbes out, for he's about six-foot-three."

"Which may be very lucky for him. But I can't see—and I'm not saying this because Mrs. Forbes has been here—that you ever had any case against him that would have had a reasonable chance of success. If he'd thrashed Coldwater rather too vigorously, and he died in consequence—that might have been natural enough. But to thrash him first, and then finish him off with a bayonet—it doesn't sound a very probable thing. But, by the way, what condition would Coldwater have been in to receive further callers after the treatment that he had received?"

"Well, he wouldn't have found it very comfortable to get up and resume his seat. His face wasn't marked, if you mean that. Forbes seems to have confined his attention to one spot. It was a case of a small man, and one about twice his size. Coldwater doesn't seem to have put up any fight, or, if he did, it made no difference either to Forbes or himself."

Mr. Jellipot's imagination dwelt upon the experiences of the man who had been whipped like a child of five, and bayoneted at a later hour of the day. He said aloud, with his usual moderation of language: "He seems to have had an uncomfortable afternoon." He added: "It looks as though you've got to concentrate on the man that you haven't yet been able to find."

He roused himself to a fresh animation to say: "But there's one thing that, queerly enough, you haven't told me, and I haven't asked. If anyone rang the bell and got no answer, it's a fair assumption that Coldwater was dead then, but how long was it before the body was found, and by whom?"

"Well, it was like this: there's a woman, a Mrs. Whitepepper, who lives round the corner in Cary Street, who was employed to clean up daily at Coldwater House She had her own keys, and expected to let herself in if she found the outer door locked, which she usually did on Mondays, when no one except Coldwater himself would be there, and he didn't usually stay as late as five-thirty, which was her time to arrive.

"She says she was a little later than usual, it being about twenty to six when she let herself in, having another woman with her, a niece, a Miss Whistler, who helps her in her work.

"The younger woman stayed below, filling buckets, but Mrs. Whitepepper went upstairs, and found Coldwater lying dead. She says she went straight to the telephone when she saw how he lay, and rang up for the police; and I don't doubt it was what she did, for it was barely five-forty-five when we got the news at the Yard, and I was on the way there."

"You've no reason to think she knew anything more than that?"

"Not the least. We found her quite ready to talk, but with nothing useful to say. Besides, the medical evidence was that the man had been dead for two hours, more or less, before she arrived."

"Then we can put her out of our minds?"

"Yes. There's nothing to be got there."

CHAPTER IV.

Potential Murderers

"WE can't expect to find a man," Inspector Combridge said reasonably, "if we don't know who we're looking for, or where he's likely to be."

It was a proposition to which Mr. Jellipot assented readily. "But," he said, "I hope it's not quite as bad as that," to which the Inspector replied that it wasn't as bad as that. It was a bit worse. After which he proceeded to explanation.

The list of appointments which had been found on Mr. Coldwater's desk read:

Flipp's Accounts	10:45
Lady Gleaner's Maid	1:30
Forbes	2:15
Long	3:15
Duckworth	4:00

"The man," Inspector Combridge went on, when he had allowed Mr. Jellipot time for the assimilation of this list, "kept a rather full diary, with a lot of information in it which we should have been glad to have while we could have talked it over with him, but he was discreet in his own way. He mentions people most often by numbers, or letters which may not be their real initials, and we haven't observed that he entered his appointments at all.

"Monday was his day for private interviews, as I said before, and he probably made a note of these on a slip of paper, such as the one we found, and destroyed it afterwards. As a matter of fact, there's no date on this one, but there's no doubt of what it was, as the list agrees with the people who are known to have called.

"Of course, those who were before Forbes don't come into the picture, unless they made a second visit, because when he beat him up, as he admits that he did, he certainly wasn't dead. But there's no doubt that they were there.

"Flipp is a man he employs for most of his dirtiest work. Not only blackmailing jobs, but making bogus purchases at shops he's trying to sell, while the victims are on the scene, and, in fact, anything that a decent man wouldn't do. He says he's there every Monday, which there's no reason to doubt.

"We haven't checked up on Lady Gleaner's maid yet. For one thing, there's not been much time, and it can't well be any help to us; but there's no doubt that she was there, because there's a cheque of Lady Gleaner's for a hundred pounds made out to self or bearer in the safe, dated two days before. Whoever stuck that bayonet under Coldwater's ribs saved the lady a hundred pounds, and possibly a lot more. But there'll be time for dealing with that.

"Besides these two, we know that Mrs. Forbes went there without an appointment. She says she had a legacy of a hundred and twenty pounds for which the cheque reached her on Monday morning, and as soon as she could get out she went to the bank and drew the money. After that, she went to Coldwater's office, and rang, and when he'd heard through the speaking-tube what her business was he had her up, and she paid him forty-six pounds, and had her letters back.

"There's no reason to doubt her tale. Her money was in the safe with Lady Gleaner's cheque, and it was her getting hold of the letters then from which the trouble began—that is, unless we are to say that Forbes had nothing to do with the man's death, about which I've still got an open mind.

"That brings us to his call at two-fifteen. Here, again, we know what happened up to a point. There's no reason to doubt Forbes' account of his interview with Coldwater up to when he thrashed him for not handing over letters he hadn't got. It fits in with what Mrs. Forbes says, and it's all the more convincing because we interviewed him about it before he'd had any opportunity of talking it over with her."

"You must have got on his track very quickly for that."

"So we did. There was the letter he'd written to Coldwater under some other papers on his desk. If was from the New Oxford Street Branch of the London & Northern, and when I rang up there I heard that he'd been working late, and only just left. They gave me his private address, and I got there just as he was putting his latch-key into the door.

"That's how it was, and I had a talk with him alone first, and then he called in Mrs. Forbes.

"I've no reason to doubt that he told the truth to a point—it's when you get beyond that!

"I learned from the bank that he had arranged to take his lunch hour later than usual—from two to three—and he was back punctually, but sent out for some sandwiches during the afternoon, saying he'd been too busy to get much lunch. The manager says he didn't notice anything particular about his manner during the afternoon, unless it were that he was in rather better spirits than usual, but he seemed to be in a special hurry to get home, and lost his temper for a moment when it was found that one of the counter-men couldn't balance his cash, and he was likely to be delayed in consequence."

"All of which," Mr. Jellipot replied, "is not merely consistent with his own tale, but provides very strong evidence that he is an innocent man."

"I won't argue that. I'm not trying to put it on him at all. But if he didn't, who did? We've got two more men on the list, and the first is no more than a name, and mayn't be a true one either.

"It's just there that we're stuck. None of Coldwater's employees whom we've interviewed yet admits having heard the name, and Flipp says that it's most unlikely that anyone would have been calling of whom he wouldn't know something. I've got two men now going over every scrap of writing in the office, and following up every number that had been scrawled on the telephone-pad or anywhere else, but up to an hour ago they'd drawn an absolute blank."

"Long isn't a very uncommon name."

"No. It would be better for us if it were. We found that Coldwater House was repainted by Long & Hewitt last year. We found that there's a James Long in the firm who's over seventy, and was in the office practically all day, and he had a son in the business who was killed in a motor accident three weeks ago. Mr. James Long said they might have painted Coldwater House. They painted a good many business premises during the course of the year. But as far as he was personally concerned it was the first time he had heard the name, and he should be sorry for anyone who wasted time trying to blackmail *him*."

"I think," Mr. Jellipot said thoughtfully, "that there are times when your profession must be intensely exasperating."

"We shan't disagree there. After that, we come to Duckworth. He's a mild little man. Small enough to have been the one who was seen washing the bayonet, but we can't arrest him for that. What he says is that he rang the bell and got no answer, though he went on till he was tired of standing about, because he wanted to see Coldwater particularly, as he was afraid of what might happen if he didn't.

"That may be true or false, but either way it saves us the trouble of looking for anyone who may have called after four, because, if it's true, it means that the man was already dead, and if it's false, it's about fifty to one that it was Duckworth who did the job."

"Had he any sufficient motive for such a crime?"

"Oh, plenty, I expect! Probably a lot more than he'll tell us. But if we were to arrest everyone who'd got a motive in such cases as this we should have to enlarge the docks."

"Yes. No doubt. It seems to me you've only got to find the elusive Long, and you'll have the man."

"I'm not saying you're wrong. But we've nothing really to go on, unless he's good enough to provide it himself, as they often do. And the worst of it is that Sir Henry's got it into his head that Forbes is the guilty man, and that I ought to be working up the case against him instead of looking round for someone else who doesn't exist."

"That," Mr. Jellipot agreed, "is unfortunate." He knew the Assistant Commissioner to be a man of sudden judgments not always established on prosaic bases of fact, and he knew also that Chief Inspectors cannot treat such opinions with the levity which they deserve.

"I wonder," he said, "whether it would be any advantage to ring up Sir Reginald Crowe. We have found his opinion on character before now to be very sound."

Sir Reginald Crowe was the chairman of the London & Northern Bank. He was known to have a better knowledge of his staff, and to maintain a closer contact with them, than most bank chairmen think it needful to do; and he had been associated with Inspector Combridge and Mr. Jellipot in a previous experience, the memory of which must always unite the three in more than a casual intimacy.

"Well," the inspector answered, though without enthusiasm, "it can't do any harm."

Mr. Jellipot hoped for more than that. He hoped it might do a little good. He had come, during the conversation, to a decided opinion that Basil Forbes was an innocent man. But if the Assistant Commissioner were disposed for his arrest, he saw that there was a serious danger that the young man might be on the threshold of an unpleasant experience, from which he must endeavour to save him. And every straw is of assistance to turn the scale.

He got through to Sir Reginald at once, which, as a large part of the bank's business now went through his office, was not surprising.

But he found the banker to be busily engaged, and disposed to cut him off before he had time to begin.

"Look here, Jellipot, I've got a most important conference on. I really haven't a moment to spare. If it's that Vortex muddle, you can just do what you think best. It's the kind of mess in which I'd trust your judgment even more than my own."

"It's not that at all. I shan't keep you more than thirty seconds. You've got a man named Forbes on your staff."

"Yes. Accountant at the New Oxford Street Branch. Quite a good man. What are you doing with him?"

"You don't think he's the kind of man who would murder anyone?"

"Yes, of course. Why not?"

"I mean seriously."

"And I didn't mean he'd think it a joke. What are you getting at?"

"If you can spare two minutes I'll try to explain more clearly."

"Call it four. The gentlemen who are here seem to be able to quarrel among themselves without any help from me."

With this permission, Mr. Jellipot gave a brief account of the circumstances surrounding Mr. Coldwater's violent end, and Basil Forbes' association therewith, and, having the benefit of this information, Sir Reginald answered the question which had been first propounded.

"If you want my opinion as to whether Forbes committed that murder, I should say certainly not. Not that I should blame him overmuch if he had, except for being a fool. When a blackmailer's killed it's an illegal service to the community for which a man ought to get six months' holiday on full pay. But I suppose it's no use telling Combridge that, and Sir Henry'd throw a fit.

"But Forbes wouldn't have done it. For one thing, he values his place with us, which he would almost certainly lose if he were convicted of such a crime. But there's more in it than that. Would he kill a man when he'd just relieved his feelings by thrashing him, and got him in a mood for licking his boots? I should say there would be no more unlikely time. Tell Combridge from me that if he arrests him he'll be sorry when he's discharged; and some nasty things said about the thick heads of the police, more likely than not.

"But if he must arrest him, and won't listen to wiser men, ask him not to do so till we've got the monthly balances out, when it won't be quite such a bother to us as it would now."

Mr. Jellipot translated this shrewd and characteristically expressed opinion of the youthful and unconventional chairman of the

London & Northern Bank into his own more precise ant less picturesque idiom, and Inspector Combridge said rather gloomily: "Yes.
He's right enough there. It wasn't a very likely time for him to kill
him when he'd just blown off steam in the way he had. That is, of
course, if there isn't something we don't know, that might alter the
whole deduction from what we do. I suppose I've got to go on looking for all the short men in London named Long, and then try to find
out whether they had any dealings with Coldwater. It sounds as
though, before I get through with that, I might be a lot older than I
am now."

Mr. Jellipot thought, not for the first time, that criminal investigation required qualities of mind and character which were not his.
He knew that he would be appalled by the hopeless nature of such a
task. Indeed, he would not know how to begin! But he did not say
this, being well content with the immediate object which he had
some reason to think he had gained. He replied only: "It does look
rather that way. And, perhaps, if you have any more trouble with Sir
Henry about Forbes, you might get him to have a word with Sir
Reginald. He might take more notice of his opinion than yours or
mine."

"Which," was the inspector's inarticulate reflection, "shows
what a fool he is." Sir Henry would doubtless regard any expression
of opinion by the chairman of the London & Northern Bank with the
deference which he would consider due to that of an important man.

CHAPTER V.

The Appearance of Basil Forbes

MR. JELLIPOT paused in his perusal of a title deed which he did not wholly approve. He made a marginal note, and, as he did so, it crossed his mind that Mrs. Forbes was due to appear. She was not likely to be later than the appointment which he had made. How far would it be justifiable for him to advise her to dismiss her fears? He did not think her husband was guilty. But he was not sure. He felt a greater confidence that the police were not in possession of evidence sufficient to obtain a conviction. That should mean that there would be no present probability of arrest. But again he was not sure. The attitude of the Assistant Commissioner introduced an element of considerable doubt.

His reflections were interrupted by the appearance of his articled clerk, Richard Dilke, at the door. "Mr. Basil Forbes is here, sir. He seems very anxious to see you without delay. He says he's only got about half an hour and the matter's urgent."

"You said Mr. Forbes, Richard?"

"Yes, sir."

"Isn't this the time for Mrs. Forbes to call?"

"Yes, sir. I told him you had an appointment, and couldn't he look in later, but he wouldn't take that. I didn't know whether you'd wish them to meet."

"Richard," Mr. Jellipot said with a kindly seriousness, "you are developing a discretion which should eventually produce a very good lawyer, if you should ever pass your examinations, an event which I will not entirely discourage you from anticipating. In the last fifty-eight years, I have seen many surprising things.

"No, I don't know that I do. Show him in, and if Mrs. Forbes calls later, tell her that Mr. Forbes is here, and let her wait or go, as she may prefer. Now I wonder," he thought, as the clerk withdrew, "what can have brought him here? Probably she couldn't keep her

28

mouth shut, and he's come to see what mischief she's done, and to tell me that, when he wants help, he knows how to ask for it himself. Well, that's reasonable enough, and he may be rather interesting to see." And as he thought this he rose to receive one of the largest men who had ever sunk into the comfortable depths of his client's chair.

The normal expression of Basil Forbes might have been genial, as that of largely made men often is, but he was evidently unaccustomed to self-repression, and now in a state of angered irritation which he made no effort to hide. "You wish to see me?" Mr. Jellipot enquired tentatively.

"Well, I've come here! It's about that damned Coldwater business, of course." Mr. Jellipot would give him no help.

"You wish to see me," he repeated tonelessly, "about that?"

"Alice said you'd be the one to make people see sense."

"I am afraid the lady we mention exaggerates any capacity I may have. It is not always easy to make people see anything. What sense are you anxious that they should see?"

"There's no need to fence. I know Alice came here."

"So I conclude. It might have been more discreet to let her do so a second time."

"Discreet be damned. I want the thing stopped in a legal way."

"Perhaps if you'd tell me, Mr. Forbes, what you want stopped, and how you expect me to do it?"

"I want this talk stopped in the bank that I murdered Coldwater. It would have been a lunatic thing to do. They might as well call me *non compos mentis* straight out. And after writing to say that I was coming to break his bones! It's like saying that I'm not fit to be in the bank at all. And, besides, I shouldn't have needed a bayonet. When I'd got him down, I could have twisted his neck like that, before he had time to squeal, if I'd been such an utter mug."

As he spoke, he made an expressive gesture with his hands, causing Mr. Jellipot to repeat his reflection that Henry Coldwater had had a suffering afternoon.

He asked aloud, with an inward thought that; the more this voluble young man talked, the more he was likely to learn: "You don't really apprehend being dismissed from the bank?"

"I should say not! They'd be in a mess if they did. I've been managing that branch for the last two years, and the turnover's about twice what it was. You can bet your boots Sir Reginald hasn't missed noticing that."

Mr. Jellipot, looking mildly surprised, said: "I hadn't known you were manager."

29

"No. And they'd tell you I'm not. If a customer wants some accommodation he goes to Mr. Broughton, and Mr. Broughton asks me what I think. That's how it works. And if they want to know whether a signature's forged they come straight to me. That's all the difference there is."

"Mr. Broughton being the gentleman who draws the manager's salary?"

"Yes, of course. You think I'm making a silly boast, but I thought you'd want the real facts, if you are to be any good to me."

"I think," Mr. Jellipot answered slowly, "that you are angry and excited, and putting matters rather differently from what you would do in a quieter mood."

"Well, perhaps I am. But look what I've had to stand! Alice playing the fool, and that filthy swine getting her cash, and she having had all the worry she has, and me going short of eggs for a year, and now a young cad like Binns making a joke about how soon I'll be in the hangman's shed! If I am, it won't be for any name beginning with C. It will be the letter before."

Mr. Jellipot had an orderly mind, which it was not easy to bustle. Declining to confuse himself among the many questions suggested by this extraordinary utterance, he went on: "I hope you didn't blame Mrs. Forbes for having come to see me yesterday?"

"Blame her? No. She should have asked me first. But she's got trouble enough with this thing turning out as it has. And it wasn't a bad thing to do. I'd thought of you myself, but I wasn't going to look as though I expected to be accused. Not till I heard what they're saying behind my back. Alice is one of the best."

"So I judged. But I understood that there are occasions when the maintenance of what you consider to be satisfactory marital relations requires the exercise of a certain amount of physical discipline, and that, on this occasion, she was just a little apprehensive—"

Mr. Jellipot paused in mid-sentence, and looked interrogatively at his bellicose client, who became momentarily silent. He even looked confused. Then he said: "Well, she was a sport to come, if she thought that. I told you Alice is one of the best." He had a further moment of silence which Mr. Jellipot did nothing to interrupt. Then he broke out with: "I said I'd tell you the whole truth, so it had better come out, though I wasn't thinking of this. It's true I have walloped her now and then. But we haven't been any worse friends for that, and it's done her good in more ways than one. It hasn't been what you'd call hard."

Mr. Jellipot was not instant in his reply. He wondered whether Mr. Forbes' definition of hardness were one to which his wife would agree. And when he paused, Basil Forbes, venturing farther in pursuit of the promised truth, drew out his pocket-book, and abstracted from its inmost recess a small piece of twice-folded paper.

"Besides," he said, "I've got this."

Mr. Jellipot opened it, and read aloud this surprising quatrain:

> "Though weals may rise across my thighs,
> And my '—ahem!—' may tingle,
> It's better to be whipped and wed
> Than be unsmacked and single."

ALICE FORBES

He observed that the lines themselves were in a more masculine hand than the signature, and concluded that the lady was not the author of the sentiment to which she had subscribed her name. Feeling unprepared for more direct comment, he asked: "You are a poet, Mr. Forbes, as well as being a banker, and—shall I say a man of your hands?"

"Yes. All good bankers are."

"It may be so. But it is a fact of which I was not aware."

Mr. Forbes admitted that it was not generally known. But he instanced Sydney Dobell, Samuel Rogers, and other bankers who had won fame for their metrical compositions in earlier centuries, to which he added a surprising list of living bankers who had demonstrated their proclivity by the publication of volumes of verse. He pointed out that he had not said that all bankers were good poets, but that all good bankers were poets, which Mr. Jellipot recognised to be a proposition less inherently improbable, and far harder to overthrow.

"You expose my ignorance," he said, "in more ways than one. But we must not allow ourselves to be diverted from the subject on which you called. I am not sure that the rather surprising sentiment which your stanza expresses constitutes a necessary antithesis, and it is therefore open to the criticism that it is not logically sound. Apart from that, there must—you will understand that I am speaking quite impersonally, so that the idea of assaulting me need not arise—there must always be the question of duress to be considered in appraising the inferential value of such a signature. But having said that, I will add that I am personally satisfied, from a remark made by Mrs. Forbes herself, that what you have said is substantially true." His mind wandered against his will to consider the probable reaction of that shrewd and capable Quaker lady, Miss Patience Manly, towards whom matrimonial intentions had been vaguely and timidly forming in his own mind,[2] if he should propound to her the propriety of signing a duplicate of that submissive poem, and withdrew baffled from that which was beyond human imagination. He ended with: "It is a world of interesting and surprising differences," and as Mr. Forbes showed no disposition to discuss this dictum, Mr. Jellipot recognised a concluded subject, and said: "I wish you'd tell me how you came to know that Coldwater was blackmailing your wife, and what you meant to do besides breaking his bones when you called upon him."

"I didn't say I should break any bones. Not unconditionally, that is. I said I should break every bone he'd got, if he didn't stop baiting my wife, and hand over whatever letters he'd got of hers. It isn't likely he'd have made an appointment if I'd put it the other way."

"No. That's reasonable. It's rather surprising that he did see you under the circumstances, not having the letters to show."

"Yes. I've thought that. But I don't suppose he took what I said literally."

"No. And I suppose he hadn't met you before?"

For the first time a smile appeared on Basil Forbes' angry countenance. He looked down complacently on his own bulk. "No," he said, "I don't think he had. But I think there was another reason that gave him confidence, and that was that he really hadn't got the letters, and could deny it with truth, knowing that he'd have Alice to back him up, whether she admitted having had them returned to her, or denied the whole thing."

Mr. Jellipot recognised both the psychological subtlety and soundness of this theory, and for the first time the possibility that Mr. Forbes had not gone beyond fact when he had described his services to the London & Northern Bank entered his mind. Well, all the better if so! Basil Forbes was clearly an unusual type, but he was not therefore necessarily a fool, and if he had wit he might be the easier to extricate unharmed from the unpleasant position in which he stood. He said: "But what I asked was how you came to know what Coldwater was at."

"It was just a letter I opened casually. I wasn't spying. I didn't think that Alice had any secrets from me. And when I'd read it, if it didn't blow the whole thing wide open, it was enough to show what Coldwater was at, and that he needed taking in hand in the right way."

---

[2] See *The Jordans Murder*.

"I shouldn't have thought that the man would have risked writing on such a subject—not so that it could be understood by a third party."

"But it wasn't from him. It was Alice's own letter. She'd been finding it more than she could do keeping up the pound a week out of the housekeeping money, and got two or three pounds behind, and into some debts with the shops that she knew I didn't allow—it was about that, more than anything else, that we had one or two differences the first year we were married, and I had to make her understand that she'd either have to pay cash or get hurt. I daresay it wouldn't seem to you that she'd done much wrong, but when a man's in a position like mine, where reputation counts, the tradespeople will give his wife almost any credit she wants, and it's a very dangerous thing."

"Yes," Mr. Jellipot agreed, "I can see that." He knew, as all solicitors must, how much misery, how many financial disasters and bankruptcies by which men are ruined or shamed, are caused, not by their own follies or miscalculations, but by the obstinate extravagance of wives whom they are unequal to check. Perhaps if there were more men who used the primitive argument that Mr. Forbes had found effective, it might be a happier world, and one with less work for the lawyers to do!

"Well," Basil Forbes went on, "when I'd made her understand that what we couldn't pay for we couldn't have, I couldn't complain if she sometimes said we must go without. I could see that she didn't spend overmuch on herself, and when she started giving me two eggs for breakfast instead of three, and talked about how much she had to spend on the children's clothes, I said I could live through that. I thought she was just a muddler, and it couldn't be helped, but what she was really doing was squeezing a pound a week out of the money I gave her for other things."

"So she wrote asking for time?"

"She wrote saying she couldn't possibly pay anything that week, but she'd got a hope of being able to pay the lot, and get the letters returned to her, if he'd only be patient, and not send them to me, as he'd threatened to do. She said, shrewdly enough, that he'd get nothing by that, and he could tell by what she'd paid already that he'd have the money from her, if he gave her time. What he needed was time of another kind. And when she addressed it she put Manchester on it instead of London, because she'd got a legacy in her head that was coming from there, and so it came back to me.

"Of course, there wasn't anything in the letters that Alice need have minded me seeing. She admits that herself now.

"She isn't the sort who could write anything she need mind being put into print for the world to see. I never supposed that there was. She was just sensitive about nothing, in a way that, if you know her, you'd understand." (Mr. Jellipot made no comment on this. He thought it just possible that he did. *"Basil would have laughed."* He remembered that. Clearly, silence was best.) "But you asked me what happened when I went up to see Coldwater.

"That won't take long to tell, and it would have been one of the best things that I ever did if some thick-headed fool hadn't stuck that bayonet into him after I'd gone.

"There's no sense in killing a man you don't like, even apart from the risk you run of dying a worse death because other people are almost certain to come butting in. If there's no life after this, you end his troubles, just as much as anything that that kind of dog can have of a better sort; and if there is, it's better to let him go on doing caddish things and warming up his last residence all the time.

"But what happened was this. He told me that it was true that Alice had had some correspondence with him, and he had kept the letters—out of affection, he was fool enough to pretend, as though I should believe that!—but he said he hadn't blackmailed her; such a thought wouldn't have entered his mind in a thousand years. He had been reluctant to return the letters because of their sentimental interest, and she had unfortunately misunderstood him, and thought that money would persuade him to give them up. If he hadn't tried to hand me that dope, I might have been easier to persuade that he'd given her the letters that morning, or if he'd said that she'd paid him over fifty pounds, though I mightn't have left him then till he'd coughed it up. He may have had the sense to expect that, or simply been afraid to admit that he'd been blackmailing her, but anyhow, he said that he'd given them back out of pure goodwill, and I told him to cut that tripe, and hand them over in thirty seconds, or he'd be a sorry man.

"So when he said it again, I picked up his chair by the back—it wasn't heavy, even with him on it; his furnishing was all about as mean as himself—and shook him off on to the floor.

"Then I sat down on it myself, and picked him up by the coat-collar, and shook him till he went quietly over my knee. There was a ruler from the desk that did well enough, and I gave him a bit of what he deserved.

"But when I found that however hard I laid on he wouldn't change from squealing that Alice had got the letters, I began to think that it just possibly might be true, so I said I'd find out, and if it wasn't I'd come back and do a more thorough job.

"I'd been mad at first, because I'd set my mind on getting the letters, and giving them back to Alice myself, with a warning not to keep anything from me again. It wasn't at all the same thing for her to have got them back a few hours before. But beating him in the way I had made me feel a lot better, and I was in good spirits enough till I met that damned detective at the gate when I got home, and learned that the man was dead."

Mr. Jellipot, who had listened very intently to this narrative, now considered it in a thoughtful silence.

"I suppose," Mr. Forbes broke out with an irritation that an inward nervousness may partly excuse, "that you're going to tell me that you don't believe anything that I've said."

"On the contrary," Mr. Jellipot replied placidly, "I am very much disposed to believe everything that you have told me at this somewhat ferocious interview. But it was not quite what I had expected to hear."

"And may I ask where it went wrong?"

"I rather thought that you had chastised him with the bayonet."

"And then stuck it into him by mistake? I suppose you'd got it all worked out to end up with me in the condemned cell?"

"No, I can't say that I had. I am puzzled by the washing of the bayonet—by it being done in the yard. I don't understand it at all. If you tell me that you did nothing with the bayonet, I am disposed to accept your word."

"Well, you can have that. I didn't even see it was there. But it's bad luck for me to hear you say that."

"May I enquire why?"

"Because I'm depending upon you to find out who did it."

"I don't think you must do that, Mr. Forbes. I'm a busy man. And, besides, I should almost certainly fail."

"There'll be no peace for me till it's cleared up."

"You don't think that it would be any help to you if I were to write to the young man Binns, requiring an apology, or threatening him with a slander action?"

"Not much. What would an apology be worth that he didn't mean? I'll tell you what I'll do. I'm not a rich man, but we can find fifty or sixty pounds, from what's left of the legacy that Alice has just had. I don't mind offering half of that as a reward to anyone who'll start us off on the right track."

"I think that might be a wise course. Say twenty-five pounds. It is not an excessive sum, but it is one for which people will usually tell anything that they have seen, if they have no very urgent reason for silence. It should, I think, be offered through the police. The trouble will be how to word it, and to avoid being worried with doubtful or bogus claims. How would you like it expressed?"

"I'll leave all that to you, if you don't mind."

"Very well. I will undertake that. And now, if you don't mind, I will ask you to go. It is, if I may mention so small a matter, a little past my usual lunch-hour, and I am afraid to think how many callers may be waiting to see me now."

Mr. Forbes rose in haste. "Holy Moses!" he said, "I've been here two hours. And I was due back more than an hour ago."

"I don't think," Mr. Jellipot said, "you need worry much about that. I will mention the matter to Sir Reginald, attributing your delay to my own prolixity, of which I have heard him say that he is already sadly aware."

CHAPTER VI.

THE INGENUOUSNESS OF BOB LONGWORTHY

INSPECTOR COMBRIDGE, returning to Scotland Yard from a vain search for elusive Longs, was informed that the Assistant Commissioner and Superintendent Davis had expressed separate desires to see him. He recognised that the difference was likely to be that between hindrance and help, but an Assistant Commissioner, even of the more incompetent type, still *is* an Assistant Commissioner, with power to do much good, or even definite harm, to the career of the most capable of Chief Detective-Inspectors.

"Let Superintendent Davis know that I'm with the Chief," he said. "I'll be with him as soon as I get away."

He found, which was not an infrequent experience, that Sir Henry was an angry man.

"I can't think," he said, "how you could let that reward-bill go out without my knowledge—without consultation with me. It was a most imprudent, improper step! You must withdraw it at once."

"I'm sorry, sir," the inspector answered mildly. "I couldn't see that it would do any harm. Superintendent Davis saw it. I think he'll tell you, sir, that he thought it was a good move. And its wording—of course, we altered it a bit, just to show that we have our own ways in these matters—but it was very carefully drawn by Mr. Jellipot. And he's a very capable solicitor, as we've found before now."

"I don't like Mr. Jellipot."

"No, sir. He's annoyed me before now."

"Yet you let him and his criminal client make cat's-paws of us in this highly reprehensible manner."

"I'm afraid I didn't look at it quite in that way."

"Don't you see that it's only done to turn our eyes from the real criminal?"

"I see that that is quite possible. But, even if that's so, it's the making of the offer that's so astute. Superintendent Davis said that if we refused to advertise the reward, a good counsel would be able to make more of it than if we did."

"Never mind Davis now. I suppose you've got a mind of your own. If there's really a man named Long, it's up to you to find who he is, without letting the murderer advertise a reward. It makes us look absolute mugs, besides—"

Sir Henry's exclamatory voice became still, perhaps because he was not sure of what, if anything, he had meant to say. His reserves of thought were always meagre, and his sentences liable to die out abruptly, like a river in a dry land.

Inspector Combridge, knowing he played a game that patience would often win, went on quietly: "You see, sir, it's almost certain that there is a man named Long, and, if Forbes is bluffing, he runs the risk that he turns up, and what he says may be bad for him. If we'd refused to advertise the reward, he'd have had that against us, and brought it up at the wrong time that we'd meant to fix it on him, and wouldn't look anywhere else. But when we do what he asks, if that's how it is, we've done better to call his bluff, and it may end in getting just the extra proof against him that we require."

"It may do all sorts of things," Sir Henry replied obstinately, "but it's more likely it won't. And what I want you to understand is that I should have been consulted first."

What Inspector Combridge understood was that the reward-bill was not to be withdrawn, but that he and Superintendent Davis were to be held responsible for any untoward development. He was too used to that to feel any particular anxiety, especially with Davis at least equally involved.

He repeated that he was sorry, which was the most frequent expression with which he left the Assistant Commissioner's room, and went off to what he hoped might be a more fruitful conference.

He found that the superintendent was not alone. A young man of slender proportions and a fresh, ingenuous primness of countenance sat on a chair opposite Superintendent Davis's desk, nursing a bowler hat on his knee.

"This young man," the superintendent announced, with a ponderous sarcasm that seemed to leave his victim passively unaware, "who is at present nameless, has called to ask us a few questions."

"Such as—?"

"He is particularly interested to know the exact conditions under which the reward in the Coldwater case will be paid. I thought, as you know Jellipot, and I don't, that you might be able to answer that better than I."

"I don't think there need be any difficulty about that. He doesn't require information that will lead to someone being found, or evidence that will secure a conviction, as these offers most often do. If the offer brings in any information that satisfies us that the murderer can be identified, or even that Coldwater was alive after 3:00 P.M., I think he would be willing to pay."

The young man brightened so visibly at this assurance that Superintendent Davis thought it well to emphasise the condition it bore. "Satisfies us, my lad," he repeated with slow emphasis. "You understand that? Satisfies *us*?"

"Oh, I could do that! When would it be paid?"

"It would be paid at once," Inspector Combridge replied. "There'd be no doubt about that. What have you got to tell us?"

"I saw Mr. Coldwater myself at a quarter past three."

"You saw him alive?" Superintendent Davis asked.

"Yes."

"And left him in the same condition?"

"Left him? Oh, yes. Of course. It isn't likely that anyone would have killed him while I was there."

"And your name is, I suppose, Long?"

"It's Bob Longworthy."

The superintendent looked at his brother officer to say: "It appears to be a case of abbreviation." He resumed his examination. "About how long were you there?"

"I couldn't say that exactly. It seemed quite a long time."

"Half an hour?"

"Well, hardly that."

"Ten minutes?"

"I should think it was more."

"You had an appointment with him?"

"Yes. For three-fifteen."

"And you kept it punctually?"

"Yes. I waited by the clock at St. Stephen's Church till it was twelve minutes past. I didn't want to be late."

"I suppose you went to pay him some money?"

"Oh, no! I haven't got any. I mean, not worth talking about. Not to a gentleman like him."

"Gentleman? We shouldn't have called him that. Why did you go to see him, if it wasn't anything to do with money?"

"I'd rather not say that."

"I'm afraid you'll have to. That is, if you want to see any money from us."

39

"That isn't what you promised. I thought I could have trusted you, being police. I thought you were sure to be moral men."

Bob Longworthy's face had flushed with some uneasy emotion. He twisted his hat nervously in his hands. There was an expression of sheep-like obstinacy on his face which warned the superintendent's long-experienced mind that he must play him without jerking the line. He said: "Now look here, son. I don't suppose you've done anything seriously wrong, and if not you've got nothing to fear from us. Even if he had found you out in something you'd rather keep as quiet as you can, you needn't be afraid of telling us here. We're not after you. We want to find the man who killed Coldwater, and anyone who can give us information that helps us in that is doing a public duty, and we shall protect him as far as we possibly can."

"I don't know who murdered him. I never said I knew that."

"No. You didn't. You said you saw him alive at three-fifteen, and left him so, say at three-thirty. If that's true, it's very important to us. It lets one suspected man out entirely, and gives us the time, within half an hour, when the murder occurred.

"But you've got to satisfy us that you're telling the truth, neither more nor less, and you can't do that unless you are quite frank as to why you were there, and what happened."

"I don't see that. I should have thought it was more like the other way."

Superintendent Davis considered this unexpected retort, and saw more weight in its simple shrewdness than he felt it expedient to admit. Was a man's statement on such a matter really less worth belief because he declined to add information on his separate and most private affairs? None the less, he meant to get the whole truth if he could.

He put an additional gravity into his voice as he went on: "Now, Mr. Longworthy, you must try to put yourself in our place, and see where you stand. You come here and tell us you were with this man at half-past three, on some business that you don't want the police to know; and at four o'clock he was dead. Don't you see that you may be in a very serious position yourself, if you fail to satisfy us that you are telling the simple truth, neither more nor less?"

Inspector Combridge, listening silently to this dialogue, and watching Bob Longworthy with the intentness of a waiting cat when a mouse hesitates to advance, saw that he understood, and was scared by, the implication of this question. His hands trembled upon the brim of the moving hat, in his eyes were visible tears. He said: "I shouldn't have come here if I'd done that. Nobody would."

"On the contrary, it might be the safest thing you could choose. Coming to us before we had run you down, as we should have been certain to do.

"Now understand that I'm not suggesting that you killed Coldwater. If I thought that, I should be talking to you in a different way. What I say is that when you tell us you left him alive you're saying something that you can't prove, and you must therefore satisfy us, if you can, that you're telling the whole truth. Can you give me the name of any living person who knows that you left Coldwater alive?"

"Mother does."

"You mean that your mother was with you, or only that you told her the same thing that you're telling us?"

The question, simple though it might sound, reduced the boy to a moment of silence. Had the criminal, Inspector Combridge wondered, really walked into their arms in this unlikely guise? Anything less like a murderer he had seldom seen. But then, he had to remind himself, that is how murderers mostly are!

After this pause of hesitation, the answer came: "Mother saw him after I left."

"Your mother saw him after you left? How do you know that?"

"She told me so when she got back."

"At what time was that?"

"Just a few minutes after me."

"Well, that's certainly interesting. We shall have to hear what she has to say."

"I'm not sure," the boy said dejectedly, "that I ought to have mentioned her. She won't want to be mixed up in a thing like this."

"You did quite rightly. It would have been bound to come out, first or last. Do you still refuse to say why you went to see him?"

"I went to appeal to his better nature."

"His *what*? And you found it a tough job?"

"I don't know that I'd done much good."

"And what did you appeal to his better nature about?"

"That's what I don't think that I ought to say."

"Don't you? Well, that can wait. We'll have a proper written statement now of what you *do* condescend to tell us."

"And then shall I have the reward?"

Inspector Combridge had risen during the last exchanges of this conversation. He had given a questioning glance to the superintendent, and received a slight nod in response. It was in both their minds that if the boy's mother were interviewed before he could return to tell her what his own narrative had been, it would be conducive either to the elucidation of truth, or the exposure of an equally possible mendacity.

Now it was the superintendent's turn to look interrogation, and Inspector Combridge answered the question: "Yes. We can promise that. Jellipot won't jib when he knows we've learned enough to clear his client. That's what he's after. I'll see that you get the cash."

He waited only long enough to hear the boy dictate his address: "6, Amptill Terrace, Bayswater," and went out to call the fastest available car, in search of a Mrs. Longworthy whom he was not likely to find.

CHAPTER VII.

MRS. RENSHAW SPEAKS FREELY

INSPECTOR COMBRIDGE pressed the bell at 6, Amptill Terrace, and the door opened with as much promptitude as can reasonably be anticipated in the Bayswater district. No. 6, Amptill Terrace—the same would have been true of 16 or of 66—was a warren of the "service flatlets" in which so many thousands of Londoners are content or constrained to dwell.

The brisk, rather slatternly, Irish maid who opened the door looked blank at the mention of Mrs. Longworthy, and said that there was no one there of that name. Was she sure of that? Yes, quite. She was evidently impatient to close the door, which, in view of the fact that it was then 11:43 A.M., the amount of upstairs work she had still to do, and the fact that it was her afternoon out, was a natural attitude.

But Inspector Combridge showed no disposition to go. Was he wrong in the number? No. He knew it to be a kind of mistake that he did not make. Had Bob Longworthy forgotten the address of his home? It was an improbable error. Had he erred as to the existence of his own mother? It was even less likely. Had he told a concocted tale and given a false address, thinking that there were few ways in which £25 could be so easily earned? It was a possible solution, and one of which, if it were true, Superintendent Davis should be promptly informed. He said: "I think I'd better have a word with the manageress. Perhaps you'll give her my card."

The girl looked at it, abated her previous brusqueness, asked him to step in, and left him seated in the hall, while she went for her mistress. The manageress, a Miss Williams, a pleasant, brown-eyed Welshwoman, quickly appeared. The brown eyes were opened rather more widely than usual, with the vague apprehension that is commonly roused by any contact with the police in the minds of those whom it is their mission to guard. She thought it to be no more than a discreet demonstration of untroubled conscience to assume, before he could speak himself, that he came searching for rooms. She said: "I'm sorry, but I'm afraid at the moment I'm full up."

"I don't wonder at that," he answered affably, looking round at the neat cleanliness of the hall, "they're not all as well kept as this. But I'm not looking for rooms."

She was visibly pleased at the praise he gave, and to find that he addressed her in so friendly a tone. She answered: "Well, you see, we've only just opened here. It's all new."

So it was. What these places would be like after five years of miscellaneous tenancies—! But he saw that he had put her at ease, as his object had been. He said: "I was told that Mrs. Longworthy lives here. It's she that I was wanting to see."

"I'm afraid you've come to the wrong house. There's no one of that name here."

"I don't think I have. It's not my mistake, if so. Have you got a young man here named Bob Longworthy?"

"There's a young man named Bob. He's Mrs. Renshaw's son. I hope he hasn't done anything wrong?"

"Is he the sort that you'd think might?"

"No. I should have thought it very unlikely indeed. I should call him a very harmless young man."

"Does he twist his hat in his hands when he sits down?"

"I can't say I've seen him. But it sounds what he'd be likely to do."

"I think I'll see Mrs. Renshaw, if you don't mind."

"Very well. If you'll wait a moment I'll let her know."

"I don't mind announcing myself."

"I don't think I could let you do that. It won't take a moment to call up."

Inspector Combridge recognised that, as he was ignorant of the number of the lady's room, it was a point which Miss Williams must decide in her own way, and in fact, the delay was as momentary as she had foretold. Mrs. Renshaw said she would receive her visitor, and Norah was deputed to lead the way.

She led up four flights of stairs that, from being easy and broad, became steeper as they ascended past landings of diminishing size, until they came to a top floor which, unlike those beneath it, had been converted into a single flat.

It consisted of two bedrooms, the larger of which was used as a living room also during the day, a bathroom, and kitchenette.

The living-room, into which Inspector Combridge was shown, was occupied by two ladies, the elder of whom rose to receive him with the remark: "Please take a seat. I think I can guess why you have called. Jessica, if you hurry, there'll just be time for you to get to the cleaners and be back when lunch is ready."

Jessica, a girl of not more than eighteen or twenty years, said: "Yes, mother," and rose obediently. Inspector Combridge concluded that conversation was not to begin till she had gone, and remained observantly silent.

Mrs. Renshaw, if that were her true name, impressed him favourably. Her eyes, like her words, had been simple, direct, sincere. He felt that, whatever the truth might be, he would have it—or at least so far as she might know it—from her.

He thought he recognised in the simple, wholesome sincerity of a face that was no longer young an evident likeness to the young man of another name. But, curiously, the girl who had called her mother did not impress him in the same way. She had a nervous, thin-featured face, such as will change from beauty to ugliness with a changing mood, and in her eyes there was a gipsy glint and a gipsy slant. It was a face that might become radiant with the years, or disfigured by envy or spite as it should find that life would be sweet or sour. But it was hard to think of her as being united by any tie of blood to the older woman.

At the moment, it seemed that she found life sour rather than sweet. It was not hard to see that her eyes had been reddened by recent tears. Inspector Combridge, an observant man, and of some domestic experience, decided, without a too-direct glance, that she would have a child in about five months. Or perhaps less.

He observed also, upon a small open desk, which would have been within reach of his outstretched hand as he sat, an envelope addressed to Miss Jessica Lee, in a girlish hand. How many names did these people have?

He was puzzled by these observations, but not displeased. It was all rather queer, but his experience was that, when you investigate murder, queer things are very frequently found. It encouraged him to hope that he was ploughing a fertile held.

By this time the girl had parcelled a dress with which her errand was evidently concerned, and as she went out, Mrs. Renshaw began to speak: "I suppose it's something about Mr. Coldwater that's brought you here. I thought that might be over, now he was dead. But I suppose that was too much to hope."

"When a man's murdered, we naturally make some enquiries. We rely on everyone to tell us whatever they know that may help us to solve the crime."

"Yes. Of course I wasn't thinking of that. What is it you want to know?"

"You have a son named Bob?"

"Yes."

"He calls himself Bob Longworthy?"

"He *is* Bob Longworthy. You see I've been married twice."

"Oh!—and the young lady is also your child?"

"She is not really related to me. She is a child of my second husband, who was married before."

"I see. I was a bit puzzled when they said no one named Longworthy lived here. But, like most puzzling things, it's very simple when it's explained."

"They shouldn't have said that. But I can quite understand that they didn't know. We've only been here a short time, and of course we just call him Bob."

"Yes. That's clear enough. The fact is that your son has come to us, and claimed the reward."

Mrs. Renshaw looked surprised. She said: "What reward? He didn't say anything about it to me."

"There is a reward of twenty-five pounds offered for information concerning the Coldwater murder."

"You mean he has claimed that? I should be surprised if, from what I know already, he could be of much assistance to you. He means well, but what he does is not always wise. I suppose he thought the money would be very useful to us at the moment. What is it actually offered for?"

"It would be paid, amongst other things, for definite proof that Henry Coldwater was alive after 3:00 P.M., which would prove the innocence of a man who is under suspicion now."

"You will excuse me saying that it doesn't sound a very large amount, if it's as important as that. I thought that when the police offer rewards in such cases they name really substantial sums."

"It's not offered by us. It's by the suspected man, and I believe it's all he can afford."

"Then we ought to help him in any way that we can, though I'm not sure that it would be very nice to take his money for that. What has Bob told you already?"

"He referred us to you."

"He didn't call on you to refer you to me. He must have said something first."

"He said that he'd seen Coldwater after three, and that you could prove that he had left him alive."

"Left him alive?" Mrs. Renshaw's face broke into a smile, though she had shown no levity in her previous attitude. "You weren't wondering whether Bob killed him, were you? You don't know Bob!" She added, with a resumed seriousness: "But he was right when he said that. I saw Mr. Coldwater after Bob must have left, and he was certainly alive then."

"You are sure it was after?"

"Yes. I think that's practically certain, by the time I got home." She thought a moment, and said with finality: "Indeed, it's absolutely certain, because he mentioned Bob having been there."

"And he couldn't have returned?"

"I came straight back here, and he was home when I arrived. No. It's quite impossible."

"That seems to let him out finally. I don't mean that we were really suspecting him. But we like to avoid assumptions for or against, and clear everything up as it comes. Actually, we've got the time of the murder fixed by these enquiries within half an hour, which is something definite, though it leaves a lot to be done.

"But there's one thing, Mrs. Renshaw, I'm bound to ask, that your son seemed very unwilling to tell. That is, why you were both calling on Coldwater within an hour of his getting killed. I'm quite willing to believe that it had nothing to do with the murder, in which case it will be absolutely private with us, but you can see that it puts the whole thing in a different light, if there's no mystery about that."

"Yes. I see that plainly enough. As a matter of fact, when I let Bob out, I suppose you might say I let myself in, as being the last who is known to have seen Henry Coldwater alive. But I'm afraid I shouldn't have been much use with a bayonet! I suppose Bob refused to say anything?"

"He wasn't at all willing to speak about what his business was."

"Naturally not. That's why I wish he hadn't gone to you at all. But I think you will have to know."

"I am sure you will find it the wiser way."

"Well, anyway, here's the tale. Last March Coldwater sold us—sold Miss Lee, really—Jessica—a stationery business off Edgware Road."

"And I suppose it was no good?"

"No. That would be going too far. We paid a great deal too much for it. It took not only a sum of money that Jessica inherited from her father when she was eighteen, but every penny that I could raise as well. But I don't think he meant to cheat us more than such a man normally would.

"The business was for Jessica to manage, and it will be all right in the end, but it will take time to work it up, and money to get the right stock in place of the rubbish there was—and that's why we're living here."

"And I suppose you were trying to persuade him to return part of the sum your daughter had overpaid?"

"No. We shouldn't have been quite as silly as that. The matter developed in a far more serious way.

"It's true that we complained when we found that the turnover was much less than we had been told. But he said that was because of Jessica's inexperience. He professed to be honestly concerned, and said he'd look in as often as he could, and give her some good advice.

"He looked in a good many times, Jessie's told me since, and persuaded her that he was going to marry her—I suppose you've seen enough in your profession of how foolish a girl can be—and the end of it is that she'll be having a child."

"And it was about this that you were both seeing Coldwater that afternoon?"

"I went as soon as Jessica told me what Bob was up to. I meant to put a stop to any mischief that he might do."

"Mischief? Do you mean violence that you thought you might be in time to prevent?"

"No. Of course not. Bob went to beg him to marry her, and I went to tell him that it should never happen with my consent."

"You thought that, even under the existing conditions, you could not approve the marriage?"

"Yes. I knew enough of the man to be sure of that. Bob, as I have said, means well, but he's not always very wise."

"How did the girl feel about it, if I may ask?"

"I don't think that matters now. We can be thankful he's dead. Of course, I should have let her marry him if I had known how he would end. The trouble was that he might have lived long enough to ruin her life."

"She'd have been a rich woman if she had. At present the law-yers can't find an heir. It looks as though it will all go to the State in the end."

"Which may be the best way. That is, unless it could be re-turned to all the people he's robbed. I should have been sorry for Jessica to be rich on such money as that."

Inspector Combridge rose. He said: "I'm sorry that I've had to trouble you. It's very likely that you won't see me again."

He was satisfied that he had been told the truth, and he might have been better pleased with a less probable tale. Still it *did* establish the approximate time of the murder, and let Basil Forbes out. That was something gained. He must consider Duckworth again.

CHAPTER VIII.

CONSIDERING DUCKWORTH

"WELL, sir, that's how it is," Inspector Combridge said, with the exemplary patience that discreet officers must exercise in dealing with even the densest of their superiors. "Bob Longworthy watched the clock and got there exactly at three-fifteen. After that, his mother got there, and by then he'd had his talk and cleared off, and she went upstairs and had hers. If it wasn't three-forty-five by when she came away, it couldn't have been much less, and it may have been later.

"It's really the more probable guess that it was. And then, at four o'clock, Duckworth's tale is that he got no answer, and came away. And he's a small man, and a small man was seen washing the bayonet."

"You seem to overlook," Sir Henry said acidly, "that this Longworthy boy came to get the reward."

"You mean, sir, that he might have made up the tale of having seen Coldwater alive, when he found that that was what he was wanted to say?"

"If he'd found him dead, and been too frightened to give the alarm, isn't that probable?"

"But if the man was killed before then, how could he have got upstairs?"

"You don't know that he did."

"There's the mother's evidence, as well as his, sir."

"You don't expect the woman to give away her own son?"

"Well, as to that, I saw her separately, before he could get home."

"And she played her part as cleverly as a woman will? You don't suppose the boy had really started out without letting her know what he was up to."

50

Inspector Combridge avoided a direct reply to this question. It suggested possibilities which had not been absent from his own mind, though he was disposed to put them aside. The trouble with the Assistant Commissioner was that he could only entertain one theory at a time, and his unreasoned advocacy was likely to rouse opposition in more balanced minds which might incline them to press too heavily on the opposite scale.

"I thought, sir," the inspector went on, in his more deferential manner, "however that might be, there couldn't be any harm in asking Duckworth a few more questions. It seems to me that he's in a rather tight place."

"That's only if you believe Longworthy. If we detain that young man on suspicion for a few hours we may find that he starts telling a different tale."

Inspector Combridge was disinclined to agree. He thought that it would more probably be waste of time, if not worse. He wanted rather to cultivate Bob Longworthy to a fuller confidence on the assumption that what he had said already was true, and that his reluctant reticence must be overcome so that he would become a satisfactory witness for the Crown when Thomas Duckworth would be in the dock.

But he saw that Sir Henry would not lightly abandon his fixed idea that the criminal was Basil Forbes, and that the energies of the C.I.D., which should have been directed to enclosing him in its fatal net, were perversely engaged in making loopholes for his escape. He answered diplomatically: "But we shan't lose anything, shall we, sir, if we question Duckworth a bit first? We can always run Longworthy in, and the more we're sure that Coldwater was dead at four, the more we can frighten him as to his own position."

"Very well," the Assistant Commissioner agreed: "if you're set on that. But don't lose any time. One way or other, you've got to make this Longworthy boy tell the truth, and then you'll have as good a case against Forbes as any reasonable jury could wish. The most likely thing, to my mind, is that Longworthy rang and got no reply, and he and his mother made up the tale in the way he told it to you just to pick up the reward. He wasn't to mention her unless he found he couldn't pull if off in a simpler way; but that money they meant to have."

"Yes, sir. I see it's possible to look at it that way. I'll get after Duckworth at once." Fortunately, there was no difficulty about that. Thomas Duckworth was butler to Viscount Swinfield, and it was an occupation that obliged him to spend the most part of his time in his employer's house. But though this conversation took place at 10:45

A.M., it was afternoon before the inspector set out for Fitzmorton Square.

The reason for this delay was partly that Inspector Combridge (as far as the call of duty allowed) was a humane and considerate man. He did not, at this time, think of Duckworth as a murderer, but only as one against whom there was a most grave suspicion, and he had trained himself to show suspects the consideration due to innocent citizens, until his own mind was finally resolved. He had observed that Duckworth was in a highly nervous condition. The man had declined to give any indication of the object of his call upon Henry Coldwater, beyond such inference as might be drawn from the admission—or perhaps assertion would be the better word—that he had been apprehensive of the consequences of failing to secure the expected interview, and had remained so long ringing at an unanswered bell that the murdered man, had he been still alive, could not have failed to hear him.

It was an easy guess that the business which took him there was discreditable to one, if not both, of those who had expected to meet, but, if Duckworth were innocent of the murder, that was not an aspect of the matter into which it was Inspector Combridge's present business to probe. Rather he would wish to make it as easy as possible for Henry Coldwater's (more or less) innocent victims to give him the assistance his case required, without involving them in avoidable trouble, either socially or with the law.

It had been evident that Thomas Duckworth was nervous of any police interest in himself becoming known either to his employers or his fellow-servants, and he had mentioned the mid-afternoon as a time when he could most easily be interviewed in his butler's room with the minimum of observation, or interference with the duties of his employment.

But, besides this, Inspector Combridge had a more professional reason for exercising the patience which four hours' waiting required. He had put a man on the routine duty of enquiring into Thomas Duckworth's character and record, though without lively expectation of any relevant fact being discovered, and he delayed now to obtain his report.

Viscount Swinfield, a dull, wealthy, charitable, most respectable peer, was hardly likely to employ a butler of criminal antecedents or proclivities, and a personal enquiry upon the telephone had elicited that the man had been in his present position for over three years, and that his services had in all respects been such as wealthy and respectable peers require.

But now Inspector Combridge frowned as he read. Thomas Duckworth might be blameless, but, if so, he was certainly unfortunate. Officially, he was an innocent, law-abiding butler. Certainly one who would be likely to recover heavy damages should his character be attacked. But three times in the last eight years it had happened that there had been serious burglaries at the houses where he was employed. Worse than that, there had been a butler named Fender in earlier years who had had the same unfortunate disposition to attract burglars to the houses in which he served, and who had disappeared when his evidence would have been valued by the police; and the zealous officer who had undertaken the present enquiry had discovered that Thomas Duckworth, on his free days, would sometimes visit the house where the aged mother of Aaron Fender lived in a modest but comfortable retirement, without having found it necessary to apply for the widow's pension for which she was by length of years, if not otherwise, eligible.

Apart from this sinister record, it appeared that Duckworth gambled—heavily for a man in his position—on the turf. He had accounts with two well-known betting firms. They had been open for several years, during which losses had always been, though not always promptly, paid. At present, both accounts were in order. Actually, he had backed a long-odds winner with both firms, and received substantial payments during the last ten days.

"Well, he's a wrong 'un, right enough," Inspector Combridge concluded, as he digested this information, "though he seems to have gone straight enough since he got into his present job. Probably thought the game was too risky to try again. Just the sort of man that you'd expect to be calling at Coldwater House. But it doesn't follow that he'd kill anyone. He doesn't sound quite the type. Though a heart-to-heart talk, with this to go on, ought to find him rather more communicative than he's been yet."

So, with a determination not to be satisfied with less than a frank explanation of Thomas Duckworth's business with the dead man, Inspector Combridge found himself seated in a very comfortable butler's pantry, as a clock on the mantelpiece, between himself and an uneasy host, struck half-past three.

CHAPTER IX.

The Stubbornness of Thomas Duckworth

INSPECTOR COMBRIDGE, confronting Thomas Duckworth, was aware that he dealt with a nervously frightened man. But he had learnt more than once before that one in such a condition may be both wary and shrewd; and in this case he knew that there might be causes to account for such nervousness other than that of having any complicity in Henry Coldwater's death.

He experienced this wary shrewdness almost immediately when he tried the effect of introducing Mr. Duckworth's earlier and probably more authentic name. He thought, with some reason, that, whether the man should admit or deny it, the fact of having been obliged to adopt either of these dangerous alternatives would further weaken any remains of self-confidence that he might possess. But when he said, with an abruptness meant to be disconcerting: "—or Mr. Fender, as I believe you are sometimes called," the man stared at him blankly, and asked: "Who by?" which left the imputation neither admitted nor denied. And while Inspector Combridge had a moment of hesitation as to whether he would do well to develop this line of attack further, Mr. Duckworth countered boldly enough with: "See here, officer, I don't know why you come after me, or what you think that you're getting at, but if you're hoping to show that I killed Coldwater, when I did no more than ring his bell, and came away when I couldn't get any answer from him, you're trying something you can't do, and you can't expect to get any help from me."

"We've just got this on you," the inspector answered with an equal bluntness. "There's a witness to prove that Coldwater was alive at three-forty-five, and you say you called on him at four o'clock, and it's quite plain that he wasn't alive after that."

"Then I should say that if you found someone who says he was alive at a quarter to four, you've found him as did him in more likely than not."

"You must leave us to judge of that. But look here, Duckworth, we only want to get at the truth. And if you've told it, you've got very little to fear, unless you keep something back. And if it's true that the man was murdered just before you got there—I don't say he was or wasn't, but I'm not putting it on to you yet, or I shouldn't be here talking the way I am—you'll have to go into the box to say when you called, and I needn't tell you that whoever's defending the man we accuse will want to know what you were doing there."

"Well, so he might. It doesn't follow that he'd find out."

"You'd be in a very unpleasant position if you didn't tell—or if you made up a tale that wasn't good enough to go down. Of course, if you tell us first, we may be able to give you some help when the time comes—there's such a thing as counsel agreeing not to ask something awkward if there's a good reason shown—but if you don't tell us the truth, you can't expect any protection from us."

"Well, I'll say this much. I called to get something back that he'd got of mine."

"Which I suppose you still want?"

"I didn't say that."

"Then you've had it back since?"

"I didn't say that either. I don't want any more to do with Cold-water or his affairs. Not as long as I live."

"Probably not; but you won't find it so easy to get away from it."

"And all I've done was to ring a bell, when I'd been asked to call!"

"How were you asked?"

"I don't see why I should say that. But it's not such a secret. I had a card."

"Have you got it now?"

"No. I threw it away."

"Wouldn't it have been more natural to keep it to remind you what time the appointment was for?"

"No, it wouldn't! As a matter of fact, it didn't say. I'd written to say when I'd call, and it just said that he'd be expecting me at the time I'd said."

"And you won't tell me more than that?"

"No. I don't see why I should."

"Then if you are innocent, I should call you a very foolish man."

"You can call me anything you've a mind."

Inspector Combridge went without further words. He had made a good guess that whatever Thomas Duckworth had gone to get he had either obtained on that occasion, or else subsequently, so that it was no longer upon his mind. In the first alternative, it could scarcely be true that he had turned away from a closed door, and in the second there must almost certainly be someone probably Flipp— who had assisted him in its recovery. It appeared probable that a straight talk to Flipp might be more productive than further baiting of an obstinate and frightened man. He saw that if it were true that Flipp had subsequently assisted the man to recover whatever he had called to get, it made it more probable that his tale of ringing in vain was a literal truth, and so deepened the mystery of how Henry Coldwater could have died during a time which had now been reduced to ten minutes rather than twenty apart from the extreme improbability that he had been alive when Duckworth had called, and had ignored his repeated ringing—an improbability which was increased by the medical evidence of the time when death must have occurred. But, after all, it was the truth he sought, and that could be reached, if at all, by elimination of error, even though it might seem at the time to increase the mystery by which he was confronted.

He resolved that his next morning's occupation should be a further talk with Theophilus Flipp, but when that day came it brought an unexpected item of information which turned his steps in another direction.

CHAPTER X.

QUESTIONS FOR MRS. FORBES

ALICE FORBES, after one of the worst frights that a loving woman can have, had recovered her equanimity as the days passed, and Basil came home with his usual regularity and with a contagious confidence in the decisive methods by which he had routed the suspicious nonsense of those poking police.

Normally an affectionate couple, the threat of deadly danger had drawn them into a closer and more conscious intimacy—she with the knowledge that it was her own folly, and his desire to protect her from annoyance in his own emphatic manner, which had brought that danger upon him, and he with a real and ready sympathy for the trouble which she had had (and which he believed to have been even more causeless than it was), complicated, perhaps, by a sense of masculine satisfaction in the part he had played.

It was therefore with the unpleasant shock of returning danger which she had too quickly supposed to have passed from a clearing sky, that Mrs. Forbes, as she had just settled the baby into its cradle, and was laying the table for her solitary midday meal, while the daily girl dished it up, saw Inspector Combridge opening the front gate with the evident intention of calling upon her.

She hesitated a moment what a time for the man to come!—and then, as the bell rang, she called out: "You'd better go on with what you're doing, Becky. I'll go to the door." The next moment she confronted the inspector, holding the door about eighteen inches open, but showing no intention of inviting him to cross her threshold.

"Mr. Forbes isn't in," she said, before he had time to speak. "He never is at this time of day."

"It isn't him that I'm wanting to see. Can I have a few words with you, Mrs. Forbes?"

"Yes, of course."

"May I come in a few minutes?"

"I'm sorry. I've just got baby to sleep."

Inspector Combridge saw that he was not to be received as a welcome guest. It was apparent that Alice Forbes was reluctant to admit, even to her own mind, that a subject which she regarded as closed could be reopened.

"Well," he said good-humouredly, "I can ask you here if you prefer. On Monday morning last week you drew a hundred and twenty pounds from a bank in Grafton Street?"

"Yes. I've told you that once before."

"And they paid you that sum in ten-pound notes?"

"Yes."

"Will you please tell me exactly what you did with them?"

"They were my money. I don't see why I've got to say that."

"I can't make you, if you refuse. But it would be a foolish attitude to adopt. You have already said that you paid forty-six pounds of that money to Henry Coldwater. You couldn't have done that exactly in ten-pound notes."

"I gave him fifty pounds, and he gave me four pounds change."

"Yes. That agrees with the amount of the notes found in his safe. But what I want to ask you is this—and I want you to answer very carefully, because a mistake—and a real mistake would be hardly possible—might have most serious consequences—were the notes you paid Coldwater some of the actual ones that you had from the Grafton Street bank that morning?"

"Yes, of course. What else could they have been?"

"That would be for you to say. It's only the fact that I'm asking now. You are absolutely sure about that?"

"Yes. Of course."

"Thank you, Mrs. Forbes. You may have helped us very much."

Showing no desire to prolong the conversation, Inspector Combridge went, leaving Mrs. Forbes in some doubt of the wisdom of the attitude she had taken.

As she thought it over, her mind became puzzled as to the possible significance of the inspector's curiosity on such a point. Might it be, she thought, with a sudden fear, that the identification of the notes would provide some evidence against Basil, which would catch him in a deadly, unavoidable trap? Would she learn in the coming days that she had brought him to death because she lacked the sense to refuse reply to questions the meaning of which she did not know?

With reflection, the fear passed. In the first place, Basil's innocence, to her, was a conviction that did not allow of the smallest intruding doubt; and surely, that being so, the truth should not be hindrance but help, assisting towards that exonerating discovery that would clear his name from suspicion even in foolish minds. And she knew enough of banking methods to remember that the identity of the notes could be established with ease. She had seen the clerk at the Grafton Street bank make a record of their numbers before passing them across the counter. Inspector Combridge must surely be familiar with that procedure! But then, why on earth had he come to her? She must ask Basil when he should come home this evening, as he surely, surely would.

So she told herself, having reason for her support. Yet she had some anxious hours before the time arrived at which suspense would be relieved by his appearance, or be exchanged for more definite fear.

CHAPTER XI.

A Question of Bank Notes

INSPECTOR COMBRIDGE, disregarding the fact that the hour of lunch had arrived, went on to the New Oxford Street Branch of the London & Northern Bank, and asked to see Mr. Basil Forbes. He had learnt enough of the bank routine to know that the manager would have gone out at that hour for his own lunch, and that Mr. Forbes would be in charge; which involved, among other propitious circumstances, that the interview at which he aimed could take place in the comfortable privacy of the manager's room.

As he approached the counter, Mr. Forbes, who had been given some instructions to a ledger-clerk at the back, came forward, with an expression of rather grim geniality, and said in a voice loud enough for most of the staff and some customers at the counter to hear: "Come to apologise, Inspector? I made a small bet that you would. I thought you were the sort that could be depended on for the decent thing."

Inspector Combridge, who had called with a different purpose, and to whom the idea of apologising had not occurred, took this quietly, and was fair and quick-minded enough to see that it was an interpretation of his visit for which there might be some justification.

"I'm always willing to say I'm wrong," he conceded. "I suppose you heard from Mr. Jellipot this morning?"

"So I did. Cost me twenty-five pounds which I'm never likely to see again to prove what never ought to have been in doubt in any reasonable man's head. You can't wonder if I feel a bit sore."

"It was an unpleasant business for you, of course," the inspector replied, "but you mustn't blame us too much. After all, it isn't our fault if a man gets himself murdered just after he's been thrashed."

In conceding this, he went as far as he felt able to do. The information that had come to him a few hours before had put him on to an enquiry which seemed to bring Mr. and Mrs. Forbes into the picture again, though he could not see what parts had been theirs. But if Basil Forbes were really innocent, he might be able to give him some help, to enlist which he must make a conciliatory approach. He added: "But there's something else turned up quite unexpectedly this morning, that I think you ought to know, and I thought you might spare me a few minutes."

"All right, Inspector. Come in." Mr. Forbes, whose previous manner had been designed to show the staff how absurd they had been to suspect him of Coldwater's death, rather than by any remaining bitterness in his own mind, was mollified by the tone of the inspector's reply. He led the way into the plainly furnished room which had heard so many sanguine anticipations, so many urgent pleas, so many tragic refusals of assistance at greatest needs—a bank's disposition to help being in inverse proportion to the urgency of the requirements which are put before it—and as he closed the door Inspector Combridge opened the subject upon his mind.

"I dare say," he said, "the public often think we're a bit slow, and it's true we do a lot of things that lead nowhere, which might be missed out by a clever man. But you know we reckon to take nothing for granted, and just plod along in our tin-pot way, checking everything, and hoping that we may stumble on something that will end us up where we want to get. Well, you know that your wife said she paid Coldwater fifty pounds in notes?"

"I understood it was forty-six pounds." Mr. Forbes' tone had become curt as he said this. What was the damned policeman trying to get at now? Accusing Alice of lying? Did he suppose that she'd stuck the bayonet into him in the morning, and that he had thrashed him in the afternoon without noticing it was there?

"Yes. Forty-six pounds. That's what she says. She gave him five ten-pound notes, and he gave her four pounds change. She says it was part of the money she drew out that morning."

"Well, so it was."

"We didn't doubt what she said, particularly as there were five ten-pound notes in Coldwater's safe."

"Which was what you'd expect to find."

"Yes. But the numbers of the notes aren't the same."

Mr. Forbes stared. He saw the improbability of the inspector's statement, but, being a banker, he did not suppose that he could be misled as to such a fact. He must observe an improbable coincidence of amount, if nothing more. But he was not going to admit anything, his wife being concerned. He said: "Well, it just shows he had some other notes, besides hers. I don't see what more you can make of it than that."

"No? Just the same amount?"

"I don't see much in that, being a round sum. If it had been say a hundred and eighty-five pounds it would be rather odder."

"But it isn't only the other notes being there. There's the question of what had become of hers."

"Well, I dare say there is, and I've no doubt there's an answer, too. But you won't get it from me. And if you think I'm going to offer any more rewards to save you making mistakes you never made a worse guess. I've lost twenty-five pounds that way now, and I dare say you've realised already that I'm not a rich man."

"I didn't suppose you'd do anything of the kind," Inspector Combridge answered, with difficult patience, for the manner with which he was met suggested that Mr. Forbes would require little further incitement to add another to the physical assaults which seemed to come so readily to his mind, "but I thought you might help me with some suggestions or perhaps even information as to what had occurred. I ought to tell you that I've seen your wife in the last hour, and she is definite that the notes she paid to Coldwater were some of those she had drawn that morning."

"Then, if she's told you that, I don't see that you can expect to get any more help from us."

"I'm not saying I do," Inspector Combridge answered, with his usual patient pertinacity; "and I'm not suggesting for a moment that Mrs. Forbes hasn't told me what she believes to be true—and probably is. It's not easy to see how she could make a mistake about that. But I needn't tell you that bank notes are about the easiest things in the world to identify, so that the truth, whatever it is, is sure to come out sooner or later, and, whether you could help us or not, it seemed only fair to let you know what the position is."

"Well, I suppose I ought to thank you for that. I'm sorry if my temper's a bit on edge over the whole business."

Mr. Forbes spoke with a moderation that there had been nothing in his previous attitude to forecast. The fact was that the inspector's argument had impressed him in a way that was natural to one of his profession. It was no question of theories or opinions here. *The truth would come out.* Nothing could alter that. Certainly the truth as to where those bank notes had come from that were in Coldwater's safe when he died. Almost certainly—unless they had been destroyed, for which there was no apparent reason, and which bank notes seldom are—the truth as to where Alice's bank notes had really gone. If he had confidence in her word—and he would not admit a doubt to his mind—there could be no occasion for temper or for alarm. Sooner or later, the truth would be revealed. It would be folly to anticipate it with futile quarrels or speculations which could yield nothing at all. And if Alice *had* made some incredible mistake or blunder, if she had had access to some other bank notes—but how could she? It was absurd! Well, it was a good thing for him to know what the danger was, so that he could warn her and get at the truth before it should be otherwise discovered.

His change of tone encouraged Inspector Combridge to speak more plainly than he might otherwise have done. "You see," he went on, "it was those bank notes being in the safe which was the main, if not the only, corroboration of your wife's account of what happened; and I'll own that I never doubted that they had come from her. It was no more than routine work to have the numbers confirmed, and I should have put it at about fifty thousand to one that they were part of the hundred and twenty pounds that we know she drew out that morning.

"I'm not suggesting now that every word of her account may not be true, but you'll see that the one thing that seemed to confirm it has gone. Apart from that, as she wasn't on the list of those that Coldwater was expecting to see, we've only her word for it that she saw him at all."

"Not exactly. He told me the same thing. And there was the fact that he couldn't produce the letters, even when I was making him howl. And I told you that before I'd seen her at all."

"Yes. I'm not trying to make out that what she says isn't true. But the question we're up against is, if she gave him the notes, where have they gone to, and what brought another lot there of the same amount? I can't help thinking that, if we knew that, there wouldn't be much left that we shouldn't know."

"You might be right about that. I can't say. Why shouldn't the man who murdered him have picked them up?"

"I should say it's quite likely he did."

"Well," Mr. Forbes said, with the first laugh that the interview had brought, "that lets me out, anyway. When I murder people, I'm not such a mug as to pick up the bank notes that are lying round. No banker would be, you know!"

Inspector Combridge did not dispute that. He thought, however, that it might have affected the matter had he known those notes to have been obtained from his own wife by blackmail a few hours before. Even if Basil Forbes had not made that fatal bayonet thrust, this idea was one which suggested a possible explanation, a possible deviation from exact truth in his account of what had occurred. But it was not an idea which it would be judicious to speak aloud. And if that were so, it was almost certain, after what had occurred since, that those bank notes would never be seen again. Mr. Forbes could certainly be trusted for that. Probably they had been burnt already! Inspector Combridge got up to go.

CHAPTER XII.

WHERE THE BANK NOTES CAME FROM

THEOPHILUS FLIPP lived in a most respectable South-London suburb, in a house of which (by the help of a philanthropic building society) he would become the owner in thirty years, providing that it could remain erect, and he continue his weekly payments for so long a time. He owned a modest car which would become his in less than three years under similar conditions, and with an approximately equal doubt as to whether its engine would continue to run until the final payment would become due. In short, he lived the outward life of a blameless clerk, and allowed himself to be exploited in the usual manners by which the small incomes of blameless clerks continue to swell the pockets of cleverer and less scrupulous men.

He had a young, harmless, fluffily attractive wife, and one child to testify to his present respectability. His Christian name was an open testimonial to the character of his parents and the anticipation with which they had launched him upon the world. And Inspector Combridge was disposed to doubt whether a greater rascal could have been found even among the varied assortment that populate all the jails of England. But he also doubted whether Mr. Flipp would ever be so blunderingly incautious as to join one of those segregated communities. It was this quality of caution, rather than any respect for abstract verities, or the provisions of English law, which gave the inspector some confidence that, if Mr. Flipp had any helpful knowledge concerning the origin or disappearance of either of the sets of bank notes, he could be persuaded to yield it up.

He called upon him at an hour in the evening when he would be likely to be at home, and with the thought that he might be more amenable to persuasion in the atmosphere of domesticity than in that of Coldwater House. But here he met with an unexpected rebuff.

Mrs. Flipp received him politely. She did not appear to be in any way perturbed by his visit. Her only fluttering concern appeared to be that her husband would be unable to come downstairs, as she professed certainty that he would be anxious to do. But Theophilus had a sick headache. It was a condition which might continue for a day, or perhaps two, and during that time it was his habit to remain in a darkened room.

Inspector Combridge recognised truth, and reflected that, even if Mr. Flipp could be persuaded to see him while in such a condition, it would be too good an after-excuse for bad memory or misunderstandings. Anxious as he was to progress with an enquiry on which he could at present do no more than move uncertainly, like a dog on a cold scent, he decided that he would prefer to wait until Theophilus could be interviewed in a normally lighted room.

So he excused himself to a young woman whose only aim appeared to be to prolong the conversation, with a promise to call again on the next evening, and gained more advantage from the delay than he could have foreseen, for the next morning brought information concerning the five bank notes which had been found in Henry Coldwater's safe. They had formed part of a sum of two thousand pounds which had been paid out over the counter of the Silver Street branch of the Westminster Bank against an open cheque drawn by Hamilton Hardcash, on the morning of the races at Northolt Park, less than a fortnight before.

The cashier who paid it remembered clearly that it had been presented by Mr. Hardcash's clerk, and it was a presumption approximating certainty that the money had been required for the racecourse operations of the day.

Inspector Combridge digested this information. Had the notes been paid out on the course, it might be impossible to trace the hands through which they had passed. But he knew that to be a doubtful, even an improbable, deduction. A bookmaker arms himself against the possibility of disaster which he may have skill to avoid. He may return from a day's battle of wits and chance with his own money still where he would prefer it to be, and a further supply magnetically attracted thereto. He remembered that Hamilton Hardcash was one of those who ministered to Mr. Duckworth's sporting proclivities. He decided to pay the bookmaker an immediate call.

Mr. Hardcash's suavity of demeanour might be a lie, yet he spoke no more than the simple truth when he said that he was always willing to oblige the police. If he could have made their sense of obligation heavier than it was ever likely to become, he might have saved himself some uneasy hours.

His system of bookkeeping was good. A delay of less than five minutes, during which he gave the inspector two excellent tips for the Lingfield races next Tuesday, was sufficient to produce the information that the notes (numbers duly recorded) had been paid, with some others and an odd balance in smaller currency, to Thomas Duckworth on the day following that on which they had been drawn from the bank.

Inspector Combridge did not doubt that this was the truth. It was what he had been expecting to hear. But he remarked an unusual circumstance. "I thought," he said, "you usually sent cheques in settlement of credit accounts."

"So we do, unless we have contrary instructions. But Duckworth always preferred to call in and pick up the cash. Didn't want any risk of our letters getting opened by the wrong fingers, more likely than not."

Inspector Combridge agreed as to this probability. He thanked the bookmaker for information which might be of vital importance, though its implications were not easy to see.

It seemed to be an almost certain deduction that Duckworth, having won a substantial sum, had used part of the money to redeem something of his, or which he desired to have, which was in Coldwater's possession, and which he had, either then or subsequently, obtained. But how, if at all, did that bring him under suspicion of the crime?

It might be said that the fact that the notes had reached Coldwater's safe was inconsistent with his own tale that he had rung in vain at a closed door. Yet could it be seriously theorised that he had called, paid the money, received what he required, murdered the man, and then withdrawn, without removing the notes by which his visit could be so certainly traced? Or if Coldwater had refused to give up whatever he held, which would supply some motive for violent attack, would it not be still less likely that he would have gone, after committing the crime, without repossessing himself of the money so vainly paid?

Inspector Combridge saw that these alternatives did not exhaust the possibilities of the case. He might have seen that which he claimed on the desk of the man who would not yield it with a good will. He might have snatched it from dying hands.

However these things might be, the inspector concluded that the tale of having rung at a closed door was not lightly to be believed. If Duckworth had lied about that, the truth must be something he could not afford to tell. Suspicion settled upon him, not definitely, but a darker shadow than it had been before.

Anyhow, there was more to be discovered. There was clearly a tale that had not been told. And, with those bank notes as a text for his discourse, the inspector thought it to be one that he would be able to get.

He waited till evening came, and went to pay Mr. Flipp a second call.

CHAPTER XIII.

THE CANDOUR OF MR. FLIPP

MR. THEOPHILUS FLIPP said that he was still feeling far from well when Inspector Combridge made his second visit, and his looks supported his words; but he was sufficiently recovered to be seated in an easy chair, and to endure the light on his eyes. He was, he said, quite well enough to talk, and professed himself to be as ready as ever to assist the investigations of the police.

Inspector Combridge thought that he understood the man's position. So far as he was at present able to judge, Mr. Flipp was innocent of any complicity in his employer's murder, and might be able to make no better guess than himself as to who had committed the crime. But he might be aware of much which it would be useful to the police to know, and which he might be reluctant to tell, lest he should be narrating his own rascality where he would be least willing for it to be exposed. On the other hand, he would, on the assumption of his innocence of the crime, be anxious to win the favour of the C.I.D. by disclosing anything they would thank him for telling, if it could be done without accusing himself.

In such a position, he might be tempted to conceal matters of which he thought the police had no suspicion, while he would prefer to speak openly if he saw that they were already too fully informed for denial to be believed.

The inspector saw that, if he should question him in such a way that he would deny all knowledge of the nature of Coldwater's transactions with Thomas Duckworth, he might be reluctant afterwards to admit his prevarications; and he was not trying to entrap Flipp, but to win his aid.

He therefore commenced bluntly: "What I want you to tell me, if you can, is why Duckworth paid Coldwater fifty pounds in notes on the day of the murder, and how and when he could have done that if his tale's true that he rang the bell, and got no answer."

"I don't mind telling you," he added, as Mr. Flipp did not seem instantly ready with his reply, "that I've found already that Duckworth doesn't mean to say more than he needs. But I didn't know about these bank notes when I saw him last, and I've got enough information now to make him see that he'll have to talk, if he doesn't want to end up in the dock. But I thought I'd ask you first, because I should have a good deal more confidence in anything coming from you."

The inspector, as he said this, might have had some difficulty in explaining to his own mind whether he were uttering a sincere opinion, or a mere diplomatic mendacity. But it may have been true enough, for though he did not attribute to Mr. Flipp any abstract love of veracity, or disinclination to deceive him if it could have been safely done, he judged that he would have no hesitation in giving Duckworth away if it should appear to be the safer course for himself, where Thomas Duckworth would be likely to regard the question from an opposite angle; and the soundness of his judgment was demonstrated by the event, for Mr. Flipp, after a moment of further reflection, but not of sufficient length to appear more than the occasion required, answered with apparent frankness

"Yes," he said, "I can clear that up for you, as far as the notes are concerned, and I think you'll find that he'll be ready to tell you the same tale when he finds you're on their track; and that not only because it's the true explanation, but because it lets him out of what might look a bit queer—I might say a bit ugly—if I wasn't willing to say what I know.

"The fact is that Duckworth paid me that fifty pounds on the day before—the Sunday afternoon—and I handed it over to Mr. Coldwater when I saw him on Monday morning. It was to repay a loan, as you'd no doubt guess, if you didn't have it from me."

"Perhaps you can tell me this. Did that payment close the transaction, or was Duckworth still in Coldwater's hands?"

The question sounded simple enough, but Mr. Flipp looked genuinely puzzled by it for a moment, before he answered: "I don't think he owed anything more, if you mean that. What I understood from him was that he'd borrowed seventy-five pounds, and had to return a hundred pounds in two instalments. He'd paid back fifty pounds two or three weeks before, and the balance wouldn't have been due just yet, but he wrote to Mr. Coldwater to say that he was ready to clear it up, and would call on Monday. But that's no more than what I heard from him. I hadn't anything to do with the matter myself, beyond calling to pick up the cash."

"I suppose we shall find the transaction entered in Coldwater's books?"

"I don't know. It wouldn't be in the books downstairs. I can't tell you beyond that."

"You mean it was a transaction of such a nature that it was best not recorded?"

"It was one of those things which Mr. Coldwater liked to handle himself."

"Then, if Duckworth had written to say that he would call on Monday, when Coldwater could have seen him alone, I don't see why he sent you to get the money the afternoon before."

"That was quite simple. It was a matter of having some security that Duckworth had deposited ready to hand back to him."

"And he didn't get it? I suppose that's why you didn't quite know what to say when I asked you whether the payment closed the transaction?"

"You don't miss much! No, he didn't have it then. He had it on the next day."

"Hadn't you better tell me the whole tale?"

Mr. Flipp had another moment of silence. Then he said: "There isn't really much to tell, and I'd rather Duckworth did his own explaining. But I take it that it's Mr. Coldwater's murder that you're trying to clear up now, and if I tell you that it doesn't make it likely that he had anything to do with that, rather the other way—?"

"No. I'm sorry I can't leave it so easily. As the case stands now, Duckworth is under such a degree of suspicion that we can't take the spotlight off him till we know exactly what happened, and why. But you're right when you say that it's the murderer we're after now, and we mayn't look too closely at smaller things if they help us to the right track. And if you're right when you say that the facts let Duckworth out of that, then you can't do him a better service than telling me what they are."

"I didn't go quite that far. I don't say they let him out. But they certainly don't let him in, if you see what I mean. They're quite consistent with his own tale that he rang the bell till he got tired. It's a tale I've never doubted till now, and when he came round here in trouble that night—I mean the Monday night, after Mr. Coldwater was killed—I felt sorry for him; and when I promised to help him, I didn't think I was doing anything wrong, and I shouldn't say I was now, though I dare say you'll look at it a different way."

"You say Duckworth came round here on the Monday evening? Did he speak as though he thought there'd been a murder?"

71

"He knew there'd been one. It was in the late night editions. It was after midnight when he came round."

"He must have been very anxious to see you."

"So he was. He hadn't even known where I lived. He was trying all the Flipps—there are only about four in the London Telephone Directory. But I'd better explain the whole thing. I can see it's bound to come out, one way or other, and I don't see why I should be involved more than I've been soft-hearted enough to get already.

"Duckworth came round that night to say that Mr. Coldwater had got what he called some 'jewellery' of his, which should have been handed over to him that afternoon, and it would be ruin to him if he didn't get it back at once, and without it coming to the notice of the police.

"It didn't appear to be anything to do with the murder, and as he'd paid the money, and the goods were his prop—" Mr. Flipp checked himself on the word, and substituted, "Were what he had deposited—"

"You mean they weren't his property?" Inspector Combridge interjected sharply.

"You don't miss much! I mean I'm not going to say that they were. But the end of it was that I promised to get them back for him if I could, and next night he came round again and I handed them over to him."

"Although you knew they weren't his?"

"If they weren't, I'd no doubt they were going back where they belonged. I wasn't doing anything to assist a theft, if you mean that."

"I didn't say that you were."

Inspector Combridge became silent, reviewing the probabilities and implications of this narrative, and checking it with such facts as he knew already. He decided that Mr. Flipp had been right in saying that if it didn't let Duckworth out it certainly didn't draw him into the net. If it were substantially true, as he was inclined to believe, it made it improbable that Thomas Duckworth had committed the crime, which was an unwelcome conclusion, for it was not his object to demonstrate the innocence of several people, which appeared to be all that he had yet succeeded in doing, but the guilt of one. So that it was with some inward satisfaction that he observed that there were at least two points in this plausible narrative on which further explanation could be required.

"I still can't see," he said, "why, if Duckworth had written that he was coming in to pay the money on Monday, and Coldwater had sent a postcard confirming the appointment, he needed to send you to collect it on Sunday."

"He didn't mean to have the security ready to hand over, unless he knew the money was there."

"You mean it had to be fetched from the bank?"

"It had to be brought from somewhere. I didn't know where that kind of thing was kept. But it wasn't at Coldwater House."

"But he wouldn't know till he saw you on Monday morning that the money was paid."

"Well, that was time enough, wasn't it? He always went out at midday."

Inspector Combridge had to recognise that this also was plausible. Incidentally, it raised another question of considerable, though separate, interest. Where had Coldwater gone to lunch?

He had already learned that it was not the money-lender's habit to take his midday meal on his own premises. His appointment with "Lady Gleaner's maid" had been for 11:30 A.M., and the next—with Basil Forbes—at 2:15. Assuming that the first would be over within half an hour, that left a clear two hours, in which he might have gone a considerable distance, in addition to having a leisurely meal, and been back in ample time for the second appointment.

Somewhere, in some secret depot, he had kept—no doubt with other things that the police would be interested to see—the "jewellery" that Duckworth had deposited as security for his loan; and at midday, as the hour approached when the man would be calling, he had fetched them with his own hands, trusting no one with articles of so dubious a nature, nor consenting to fetch them at all until the money had been repaid.

Well, that cleared the first point, but the second was still to come.

"You appear," he said, "to be telling me that Coldwater had this jewellery at hand, ready to be passed over to Duckworth, when he was killed, and that we either overlooked it altogether, or overlooked that you removed it on the next day. I can't easily accept that. I know how thoroughly we examined the room."

"So I've no doubt you did, but it wasn't there. I told Duckworth that I could do nothing for him if you'd found it already in Mr. Coldwater's room; but I rather thought it would be in a safe in the one on the other side of the passage, and that's where I found it. It isn't a very strong safe, but it's let into the wall so that it isn't easy to find."

"And you were able to open it?"

"Yes, there were two keys, and I always had one. I used to leave any money I had collected there, if Mr. Coldwater wasn't about, and he'd know where to find it."

"I expect there were other things there, besides this jewellery?"

"No. There was nothing else. You can look yourself, if you like." He took a key from a rather heavy bunch, and passed it over to the inspector, who accepted it without gratitude. He would have liked to see the inside of that safe on an earlier day.

"Perhaps," he said, "having told me so much, you might enlighten me as to what the nature of this mysterious jewellery was."

Mr. Flipp may have been glad to turn the conversation away from further consideration of the safe, the existence of which he had not previously disclosed. He answered: "It wasn't what I should call jewellery. Not exactly. It was some gold plate."

"Solid gold?"

"Yes."

"Doubtless bearing Lord Swinfield's crest?"

"I couldn't say about that. I don't even know what his crest is. I didn't see the plate till I got it to hand back to Duckworth."

"Well, it's plain enough, especially as we know that Viscount Swinfield was to be away for another two or three months, and came home unexpectedly.

"I suppose Duckworth's bets went wrong, and he borrowed on the security of his employer's plate, which he knew wouldn't be required in his absence. And when he heard that Viscount Swinfield was coming home he was able, fortunately for himself, to redeem it before the agreed time. I suppose, if things had gone an opposite way, it would have been dropped into the melting pot, and that scoundrel Coldwater would have denied ever having had it at all.

"But I'm not troubling about that plate now. Especially as it seems to have found its way back. Suppose Coldwater made some excuse for not handing it over, and Duckworth lost his head after a quarrel, and killed him in desperation, or revenge, or just to get the plate back, which he was frantic to have—I suppose he might have searched for an hour and not found it, where it was hidden away?"

"No. He wouldn't have found it. But I don't think it would have happened like that.

"For one thing, Mr. Coldwater wouldn't have refused. It wasn't his way. He made some queer bargains. I'm not saying he didn't. But he always stuck to them. Where would his business have been, if people hadn't known they could trust him for that?"

Inspector Combridge saw reason in this. Honour among thieves may not be practised as commonly as the proverb would have us believe, but there are some classes of illicit business which could not exist for a month if their patrons did not know that their bargains would be observed.

Besides, unless Mr. Flipp's tale were to be entirely discredited, there was the fact that the plate had been brought from its hiding-place, presumably not more than two or three hours before, for the apparent purpose of being handed over when Thomas Duckworth should call.

Add that a man who had so recently been thrashed by Basil Forbes would hardly be in condition or mood for infuriating another caller, and the improbability of that explanation became extreme.

"You can reckon," Mr. Flipp continued confidently, "that that plate would have been on Mr. Coldwater's desk about the time Duckworth was due, or a bit before, and while it was there he wouldn't have had anyone else up. The fact that it was still in the safe makes it likely he was killed by someone who called not later than about a quarter to four."

"But if we have a witness who saw him alive at about that time?"

"Then I should say you'd be talking to a man who could tell you a bit more as to how he died."

"And if that man should be a woman?"

"Then I should say she's a liar, and ask myself what man she's likely to want to shield."

CHAPTER XIV.

A Consultation with Mr. Jellipot

INSPECTOR COMBRIDGE owned to himself that he was a puzzled man. The wisdom of Mr. Flipp had been too apposite in its deduction to be put lightly aside, however little he might honour the source from which it came. Mrs. Renshaw *had* had a man—one under the very gravest suspicion, and her own son—to protect, and her evidence might be concocted to save him from the gallows that he deserved. Indeed, if she had called at Bethnal Square only to discover the corpse of the man whom her son had left a few moments before, what else would she be likely to say? But, for all that, he could neither think of Bob Longworthy as a probable murderer, nor reconcile his conduct in claiming the reward with the consciousness of having committed the crime.

He saw that all the progress he had made in the last two days— if it could deserve such a word—had shifted the spotlight of suspicion somewhat from the dishonest butler back to Bob Longworthy, or even to Basil Forbes and his wife in a vague manner, for while the origin of the bank notes that had been found in Coldwater's safe had been ascertained, the mystery of those which had been paid to him by Mrs. Forbes—for which there was no more than her own word!—remained. Suppose that Bob Longworthy, as he might have told his mother, had found Coldwater dead, but had thought that he could claim the reward most safely by making a contrary statement? Might not Mrs. Renshaw, judging better than he the folly of what he had done, have felt it necessary to support his tale? Or suppose that she did not know what to believe, whether to account her son a murderer, or to accept his statement that he had come on a dead man? Might she not still have felt it wise to resort to the same lie? And did not such a theory return suspicion to Basil Forbes to the exact degree that he was disinclined to regard Bob Longworthy as the guilty man?

76

Well, Sir Henry had said from the first that that was where the truth lay! Had he allowed Mr. Jellipot to persuade him too easily to turn his eyes away from a guilty man?

He reflected that, if Basil Forbes were still under suspicion, Mr. Jellipot's interest in the case remained. What would that astute lawyer say to these last developments? He thought it would be at least interesting to test his reaction.

He anticipated that Mr. Jellipot would still endeavour to persuade him of the innocence of Basil Forbes, but it did not follow that he would fall to the lawyer's arguments! And even if he should do so, and be proved wrong in the end, there would be some consolation in the thought that they would both be in the same boat. Mr. Jellipot would not be able to bring his surprising explanation at last, to confound the officers of the law, like a rabbit out of a hat!

With these thoughts in his mind, he rang up Mr. Jellipot's office, and learned that the lawyer would be disengaged in an hour's time and at leisure to see him.

Mr. Jellipot received him with his usual quiet cordiality, and listened without interruption to the latest developments of the case, after which he said cheerfully: "Well, you seem to be getting on! It's wonderful to me how you find out all you do."

Inspector Combridge, more conscious of being unable to find out the one thing that he sought, had a moment of angry suspicion that there was sarcasm in what he heard. But a glance at Mr. Jellipot's face, and the knowledge of him that their long acquaintance had brought, combined to put aside an unworthy doubt, while, as though having read it, the solicitor went on: "I know, if I ever commit a murder, as we are all liable to do under sufficient provocation, my first prayer will be that you may not be put on the trail. I think I should just give up trying to get away, acting like a mesmerised rabbit is said to do when it looks in a snake's eyes."

"I don't know," the inspector answered, not entirely appreciating this simile, "that I'm particularly like a snake. I've never heard myself called that before."

"And you know, Combridge, you can appreciate exactness of language well enough to understand that I haven't called you one now. As a matter of fact, if you'll forgive the idea, you're much more like a bloodhound that never turns from a scent till he's run it down. That's why I meant that I should feel no hope of getting away."

"I can't turn from a scent that I haven't got."

"You mean that you've got rather too many candidates for the dock, and you can't make up your mind which to choose. Well,

77

that's surely better than one too few! And I don't think you're on a cold scent at all. You don't know exactly what your victim will look like when you catch up, but that's a quite different matter. Every scrap of information you get must be guiding you farther on the right road, even though it's only by ruling out someone about whom you might otherwise make a mistake."

"Well, that's a cheerful way to look at it! Perhaps I shall feel more in the same mood if you can give me a tip as to who it was who used that bayonet, and then gave it a wash in the yard."

"I am afraid," Mr. Jellipot answered, "that that is more than I am able to do. I haven't your experience in these matters. And besides," he added seriously, "the trouble with me is that I haven't a quick mind. You've told me a lot of most interesting things in the last half-hour, and I dare say they would explain the whole thing to a more logical mind in less time than we've been talking now, but I might think about them for half the night and then suddenly see something that I'd missed as I'd gone over them fifty times before."

"I'd willingly lie awake all night, if I thought that would do any good."

"I've no doubt you would, but it would be a most unfair thing to expect. You have the same right, I won't say to a five-hour day, because I understand that they are mainly manual workers who become exhausted as quickly as that, but as the rest of the world to proper recreation and sleep when you've ended a fair day's work, which I'm sure you habitually perform. It would be quite different if I should think about a thing like this in the night, because it's a kind of recreation to me."

"Well, I'll be eternally grateful to you if you will."

"You mean if I should happen to light on the explanation that eludes us now? That's rather too much to hope! I will say it's becoming a more interesting case than I had any idea that it was likely to be."

Inspector Combridge felt that "interesting" was hardly the right word to use. Baffling, maddening, exasperating—surely there were a hundred more adequate to express the enigma that it was his duty to solve. If only he knew what to do next!

"I wish," he said, "I could find out where those bank notes are now that Mrs. Forbes drew that morning. I've got a feeling that, if we knew that, we should have a start on the right road."

It was an idea which he expected to be coldly received, if not warmly repudiated, as reflecting by implication upon those whose interests Mr. Jellipot had undertaken to watch, but, surprisingly, he found it to be received in a different manner.

"Yes," Mr. Jellipot said thoughtfully, "so it might. Or it might not. It's certainly one of the most interesting features of the whole business, as it stands now."

"Of course, your banker client may have had them destroyed."

"Obviously," Mr. Jellipot agreed. But he didn't speak as though he regarded it as a likely thing.

CHAPTER XV.

THE HISTORY OF A TEN-POUND NOTE

AFTER his talk with Mr. Jellipot, Inspector Combridge had a blank week. The most sedulous enquiries failed to discover any restaurant or other resort, public or private, where Henry Coldwater had been in the habit of taking a midday meal, or the place, if any such actually existed, at which he had hidden Viscount Swinfield's plate.

Convinced as he was that the murderer must be one of the three—Basil Forbes, Bob Longworthy, or Thomas Duckworth—he yet found that the more narrowly he examined the evidence against any of them, the more he was disposed to reject it in favour of one of the other possibilities, which in its turn would be thrown reluctantly aside.

To prefer the theory that Duckworth had committed the crime had the advantage of simplicity, in that it did not imply any lack of veracity in the tales told by any of the previous callers; but, apart from that, what probability was there that he should have done it? What shred of evidence was there to refute his own statement that he had rung in vain at a door which remained closed?

The case of Bob Longworthy was simpler in another way. There was an evident motive—revenge for the honour of one whom he had been brought up to regard as a sister, and for whom he might have an even stronger feeling than a brother's can naturally be—and against it was no more than his own mother's assertion. But further questioning did not avail to shake either of their testimonies in any essential particular; and in regard to that of Mrs. Renshaw, Inspector Combridge concluded that, if she had not met Henry Coldwater alive, she was about the most circumstantial and convincing liar that he had ever met.

And if that were true, he was back to Duckworth again! If he should disbelieve her, did it necessarily convict her son? No; for they might have become joined in a common lie. Basil Forbes came into the picture again. And there was that mystery of the missing bank notes to suggest that there was at least *something* more to be discovered. Something that might alter the focus of the baffling facts he already had.

And if Mr. Jellipot lay awake this week, he had no inspirations during the nights; or, at least, none that he communicated to the inspector, as it would have been an act of friendship to do.

It is probable that an impatient Assistant Commissioner would have transferred the enquiry to other hands before the week was over had not Inspector Combridge himself suggested that he should be relieved of it, on which Sir Henry's spirit of irritated contrariety had led him to say that he wasn't going to allow anything of the kind. It was a simple case enough, and he required Chief Inspector Combridge to show his competence by bringing it to a proper conclusion.

He was supported only during this time by the steady backing of Superintendent Davis, and the fact that two conferences of the higher officials of the Yard had failed to suggest anything possible that he had omitted to do, and had agreed that there was insufficient evidence to justify the arrest of any of the three suspects. In coming to this decision they had been influenced not only by the paucity of affirmative evidence; there were the danger signals, to their experienced minds, of separate circumstances for which even a sufficient explanatory theory was hard to find.

There was not only the question of the missing bank notes; there was the mystery of the man who had washed the bayonet in the yard within full view of about thirty windows, and under the possible observation of a hundred curious eyes.

And then—just a week after that talk in Mr. Jellipot's office— there came the news that one of the ten-pound notes that Mrs. Forbes claimed to have paid to Henry Coldwater had reached the Bank of England from the London Clearing House on the previous afternoon.

It was a matter of less than two hours to trace it backward to the National Provincial Bank, to a Bayswater branch, to the account of Messrs. Tyne & Whitcomb Ltd., a firm of house-agents to whose offices Inspector Combridge was soon on his way, with a suspicion growing in his mind of what he would be likely to learn.

Mr. James Whitcomb, Jr., the secretary of Tyne & Whitcomb Ltd., received him with the rather nervous courtesy with which officers of the C.I.D. are familiar, and which they learn to recognise as being no certain evidence of a troubled conscience.

81

Yes, he said, after a brief reference to his cash-book, there had been a credit of £428 5s. 8d. paid into the bank the day before yesterday. It consisted of cheques that had come in by post that morning, and of the collectors' returns for the previous day, much of which would be in cash, as it was mainly small or medium class property with which they dealt.

A reference to the paying-in book disclosed that there had been one bank note only—one ten-pound note—included in the credit. There should be no difficulty in tracing from where it came.

The collector concerned was fortunately in at the time. Mr. Whitcomb, Junior questioned him for a moment in the outer office. He returned to take up a half-sheet of note-paper on which he wrote a name and address.

"That's where it came from," he said. "Part of the quarter's rent. We sent round for it, as it was a week or two overdue, and she's a new tenant. Nothing really wrong about the note, I suppose? As a matter of fact, she had particularly good references."

Inspector Combridge assured him that there was no reflection implied in the enquiry which he was making, either upon the lady herself or the bank note which she had used to discharge her debt.

"I'm just tracing its history, and I expect I shall have to go a bit farther back than I have yet. I don't suppose you'll hear any more about it from us."

He went away feeling that he was on the track of something useful at last. The address on the notepaper was: *Miss J. Williams, 6, Amptill Terrace, W.2.*

He was received by Miss Williams herself, with the familiarity of previous acquaintance, and with more cordiality than he had met at his first call.

"You want," she suggested, "to see Mrs. Renshaw again?"

He hesitated a moment. A word from Miss Williams, admitting that it was from Mrs. Renshaw's hands that the bank note had come would be conclusive evidence of its origin, but was it likely that Mrs. Renshaw would deny that? And to raise the question at all, without giving Miss Williams a fuller explanation than he was willing to do, would be to leave a groundless suspicion in that lady's mind, which might be permanently detrimental to the relations between her and her top-floor tenant. Put it how he might, and with whatever disclaimers, the fact would be likely to remain fixed in Miss Williams' mind that Mrs. Renshaw had paid her rent with a bank note which had attracted the curiosity of the police, even though the course of the present enquiry might be such as to relieve both her and her son from any complicity in the murder.

Indeed, he might have done some unintentional harm already to Miss Williams herself. If she should be in arrears with her rent, if she should be seeking a favour of any kind from Tyne & Whitcomb's, would it not be vaguely remembered against her?—"Wasn't it from No. 6 that we had that phoney note?"—"Well, not phoney exactly, but there was evidently something about it a bit queer."

Inspector Combridge knew that such unfortunate consequences of the enquiries that it was his duty to make must be inevitable as long as men have imaginations and women tongues; but he endeavoured to avoid provision of needless fuel for idle fires. Now he said: "Yes, I should like a few words with her, if she can see me now."

Miss Williams said she would ring up to enquire, and retired for that purpose to her basement lair, from which she sent Norah a minute later with a message, that Mrs. Renshaw said she would see the inspector, if he would kindly go up.

Mrs. Renshaw received him with her usual cheerful placidity, and if a slight anxiety was also apparent, it was natural enough, and it was a feeling that she showed no disposition to conceal.

"I hope," she said at once, "that Bob hasn't been worrying you again."

"No. He hasn't worried us. Not since he picked up the reward. He doesn't come unless we send for him now."

"I think he feels that he has given you all the information that he can. He says that you have been over it with him till he's getting a bit mixed between things he really remembers and things you keep asking him if he can't. I suppose you've seen for yourselves that he hasn't got a very good head."

"Oh, I don't know. He's got some rather queer notions in it, but it's wide awake in its own way. But I didn't really call about him. The fact is that there are some bank notes that may have passed through Coldwater's hands—I don't say they did—that we are particularly anxious to trace. One of them is the one you paid to Miss Williams a few days ago, and I thought you wouldn't mind helping us by saying how it came into your hands."

As he said this, he watched for any sign of perturbation of fear, which he felt that the question would almost certainly rouse. He supposed himself to have come to one of those critical moments when the barrier of denial breaks before the pressure of the ceaseless, gradual sapping methods he knew so well how to pursue. He expected to return to headquarters with the satisfaction of being able to report that he had identified the murderer, and was in process of constructing the case against him with the meticulous scrupulosity that the law required.

For how could there be a true explanation of how that bank note had passed from Mr. Coldwater's office into this woman's hands which would not at least convict her of having told much less than the truth? And if she should lie—as she might be tempted to do, for her son's sake, if not her own—it would almost certainly be a tale that could not be sustained, and its demolition would carry him far towards the goal of legal evidence that he struggled so patiently to reach.

But Mrs. Renshaw did not look startled or fearful. She looked blankly puzzled. And the reply she made sounded incredible in itself, and yet, if it were false, of an amazing futility.

"I'm afraid you've got something wrong. I never paid Miss Williams any bank notes. She must have made a mistake if she said that."

"Miss Williams hasn't said anything—yet. I thought you might prefer that I should ask you direct."

"I don't see why you should think I have any preference in the matter. But I can tell you at once that I never had any bank notes from Mr. Coldwater in my life, and it's equally certain that I have never paid any to Miss Williams. Mr. Coldwater's dead, so I can't tell you to ask him; but Miss Williams won't be far off, and I'm sure she'll tell you the same thing."

Inspector Combridge, wishing now that he had taken that course at first, said he would, but did not instantly rise to go. He asked: "If you hadn't had any notes from Coldwater, mightn't he have paid some to Bob?" (Suppose, he thought, they should try to get out of the mess by saying that the boy had had the note, perhaps on his sister's behalf, on an earlier day, and find themselves caught in an evident lie when it should be shown that it had been paid to Mrs. Forbes a few hours before the murder occurred?)

"I'm quite sure," she said, with conviction in her voice, "that Bob wouldn't have had anything from him without telling me."

Having this confident assurance, he had a sudden feeling of sympathy, seeing that it might be here that the real tragedy would lie. How many mothers have had a similar confidence in a criminal, worthless son!

"Would you mind telling me," he went on in a more friendly voice than he had used previously, "what was the amount of the last payment you had occasion to make to Miss Williams, and at what date it was made?"

"No," she said indifferently, "if you think it's any use to you to know that. I paid her last Monday. The rent is eight pounds a month, and there were some extras. The whole account was just over ten pounds."

She turned to the bureau as she spoke, and produced a receipt for £10 3s. 7d., which she handed to him.

"You probably paid this by cheque?"

"No, cash. As a matter of fact, Bob gave me five pounds towards it from the reward money that Mr. Jellipot paid him, and he gave Jessie the rest."

"Thank you, Mrs. Renshaw. I'm sorry to have had to trouble you."

He rose to go, sorry for the woman, but undisconcerted by this unexpected check. Miss Williams still remained as an almost certain source of information, which she was unlikely to object to give.

CHAPTER XVI.

THE FURTHER PURSUIT OF A TEN-POUND NOTE

MISS WILLIAMS was passing the foot of the stairs as Inspector Combridge came down, so that he was able to ask her, without previous formality, for the information that he required.

"There's just one question," he said, "that I should like to ask, if you don't mind. You paid a ten-pound note to Tyne & Whitcomb a few days ago—a perfectly good note, there's no question about that—but I should just like to have your confirmation of who paid it to you."

"It was Mrs. Renshaw's rent."

"There's no possible doubt about that?"

"Oh, no. I think it's the only ten-pound note I've had since I opened here."

"Mrs. Renshaw paid it to you herself?"

"Yes. It came down on her tray."

"In an envelope?"

"No. I don't think so. I'm not sure. I should say there was just the bill and the bank note on it, and some loose change to make up the amount. I expect Norah'd remember."

"She would have brought it down?"

"Yes. It came down on the breakfast-tray. I'm nearly sure about that."

"Thanks. That's really all I wanted to know. What time does Bob Longworthy usually come in?"

"About five to one. He's due in about ten minutes now."

"Thanks. No, I don't think I'll wait now, thank you."

Inspector Combridge went out, having decided to spare his mother by interviewing Bob in the street.

After a few minutes' waiting, he saw him approach. A small, upright, but curiously undignified figure, with noticeably swinging arms. He did not observe the inspector until he actually stood in his way, being abstracted in his own thoughts. His face was solemnly cheerful. Perhaps sanctimonious would not be an unfair word.

An improbable murderer, Inspector Combridge thought, as he had done before. A young man with a well-developed conscience, which did not appear to be causing any special trouble at the moment. But perhaps he had persuaded himself that the avenging of Jessica's honour had been duty rather than sin?

His eyes changed their focus, and became conscious of the inspector's presence. They changed to a look of undisguised repugnance. Inspector Combridge, planted firmly in his way, thought for a moment that the boy would have attempted to dodge past him, as though not recognising who he was.

But, instead of that, he looked up to say, in a tone of weak exasperation: "I'm not going to say any more about it. Mother says I've said too much now. I can't sleep at night. It isn't fair the way you go on when I've done nothing wrong."

"I'm afraid there's one thing you'll have to tell me. Where did you get that ten-pound note from, that you used to pay Miss Williams's account?"

Bob Longworthy looked at the inspector with eyes that became puzzled, and then indignant, and then changed to an expression of fear. "I don't think," he said, "you're the one that should ask me that. You know I had it from Mr. Jellipot, and you know what it was for."

It was the inspector's turn to be taken aback by this reply. Was it possible that it was a mare's-nest that he had been hunting with such sanguine zeal?

He saw the probability—almost the certainty—that the reward which Basil Forbes had offered would have been paid from the £120 that his wife had drawn. It would be from the same series of notes. What more likely than that Mr. Jellipot should have passed on the actual ones that he had received from his own client? What more possible than that there should have been some confusion as to which five notes of the twelve that she had received Alice Forbes had handed over to Coldwater?

He would prove that, one way or other, of course, not accepting this reasonable explanation without thorough test, but for the moment he felt a most utter fool.

Yet this feeling did not prevent him continuing to probe the details of the event with his habitual thoroughness.

"If that's how you got hold of it," he said, "I can't see why you troubled to change it for the pound notes that your mother put out for the rent."

87

For the following moment Inspector Combridge was unsure whether he was to be left in that state of ignorance. The look which Bob Longworthy gave him was suggestive of a resentful and possibly rebellious sheep.

"It wasn't you who gave them to me," he said, "it was Mr. Jellipot, and I don't know why I should tell you what I do with them; but I suppose policemen can't help thinking people are always trying to do something wrong. Mother was quite right that I shouldn't have got mixed up with you the way I have. But I don't mind telling you, if you'll promise that you won't bother me any more."

"I never make that kind of promise, but if I find that that was one of the notes you had from Mr. Jellipot, I don't suppose we shall want to ask you any more about it."

"I don't see what it's to do with you whether or not. But Mr. Jellipot gave me five one-pound notes that I gave Mother to help make up the rent, and I wanted Jessie to have the twenty pounds, but she said I must have three pounds out of it for some new clothes, and I couldn't take that without changing one of the ten-pound notes, so I took it out of the rent money, and I don't see that that matters to anyone except Mother and me."

"But your mother didn't know this?"

"I don't know whether she did or not. She was in the room when I changed the money on the tray. I didn't ask her, if you mean that. There was no reason I should. I don't see what difference it made."

Inspector Combridge thought (in which he was quite wrong) that it had done nothing more or less than give him a busy and most abortive day, but he was fair enough to see that, if the boy's tale were true, the fault did not lie with him, but with whoever had mixed the numbers of the notes.

He became almost apologetic in his parting words, the doubt of whether he might be talking to the murderer of Henry Coldwater having been lost in this exasperating question of the identity of the notes; and after getting a hurried meal at a nearby teashop, he summoned a passing taxi, and gave the address of Mr. Jellipot's Basinghall Street offices.

Mr. Jellipot was in, and with no more than five minutes' waiting Inspector Combridge was shown into his private room.

"I hope," the solicitor said at once, "that you haven't come to ask me for any further help in the Coldwater case, because you won't get it from me; but if you've found anything out I shall be very interested to hear, for the more I have thought about it the more fascinating it has become."

"I've come for a bit of help that I think you'll be able to give me, all the same. But we don't call this case fascinating at the Yard. We give it a quite different adjective." It may have been the natural annoyance stirred by the thought that Mr. Jellipot was able to regard it with such detachment that caused him to add, with a sarcasm to which he was not naturally addicted: "But I thought you could always solve these little problems if you lay awake in the night, and that was what you were going to do."

"I don't think I said that; and, if I did, it was very foolish. I have given the case a good deal of thought, because it docs appear fascinating to me, though I quite see that you can't appreciate it in the same way. But I've only been able to imagine one possible solution, and that's so improbable that I don't feel that I ought to mention it, even to you. Or, perhaps, especially to you would be a more accurate description of how I feel."

"You don't mean that you'd let me flounder about, while—"

"Probably not. But before I put that particular idea into your head, I should need to give it a good deal more thought than I have yet. But suppose you tell me what it is you think I can do to help you now?"

"The point's this. The twelve ten-pound notes that Mrs. Forbes received were numbered consecutively BC/VP X 300720 to BC/VP X 300731. According to the information I had subsequently both from her and her husband—who wouldn't be likely to go wrong on such a point, particularly after he knew how important it might become—the numbers left in her hands after she'd paid Coldwater were twenty-five to thirty-one, so that she appeared to have paid him the first five numbers, which would be at the top of the roll, and that's just what would be most natural for her to do.

"Well, we heard yesterday that number 300721 had turned up at the Bank of England, and I thought that I could see a peep of daylight at last.

"We traced the note back to 6, Amptill Terrace, and I've got Bob Longworthy to admit that it came out of his pocket, but he makes no difficulty about explaining that. He says it was part of the reward that he had from you. Now what I want to know is whether you can check up on that."

Mr. Jellipot answered with precision: "Mr. Forbes gave me the amount of the promised reward in the form of two ten-pound notes, and five notes of one pound each. They were fastened together with a wire clip, and remained in the open envelope in which he had handed them to me.

"When you sent Longworthy to receive the reward, the envelope was taken out of the safe, and brought to me here. I inspected its contents, and then handed it over to Newman, instructing him to take Longworthy to the outer office, and draw up a proper receipt, in exchange for which the contents of the envelope were to be given to him.

"I have no reason to doubt that my instructions were carried out with exactness, and you can take it as a fact that the notes which Bob Longworthy received were those which Forbes brought to me. But I can't go beyond that, unless Newman has some record of the numbers, which is improbable, but about which I will enquire."

Mr. Jellipot picked up the telephone. He said: "I want Mr. Newman. Ask him to bring Mr. Longworthy's receipt for the Coldwater reward." He added, as he replaced it: "Forbes ought to be able to put you right about that."

"I've had the numbers from him already."

"It's not a point on which he would be likely to go wrong."

"Not unless he did it on purpose."

Mr. Jellipot considered this possibility. "It doesn't sound probable," he said; "particularly because he would know that, sooner or later, the inaccuracy would be disclosed, and would bring suspicion upon himself. And it seems pointless in other ways. On the other hand, Longworthy's explanation is so simple and natural that it is most probably true." He would have liked to say again that it was a fascinating case, but consideration for the detective's feelings silenced his voice. Then the managing clerk entered the room.

He laid the receipt before Mr. Jellipot, who looked at it with the natural satisfaction of a precise man who observes that the efficiency of his staff is about to be demonstrated, even beyond what could be reasonably required. He passed it over to the inspector, saying only: "That should, I think, give you the information for which you ask. Thank you, Newman. You needn't stay."

Inspector Combridge read that Robert Longworthy acknowledged the receipt of two ten-pound notes, numbered BC/VP X 300725-26, etc. He asked: "May I keep this?"

Mr. Jellipot observed that his eyes had become bright, his mouth rather grimly set. He answered: "Yes. You can have that. I suppose you think that you are hot on the track of the murderer now? I don't say you are wrong. You have compared this to the Razor Street case once or twice. You must take care that it doesn't end up in the same way."

"You mean that we made the right arrest, and the jury gave us one on the chin?"

"Yes. It would be a quite possible development. But when you compare it with the Razor Street case, you should, if you will pardon the suggestion, be careful not to overlook an important difference."

Mr. Jellipot paused as though he would choose, with even more than usual deliberation, the words which his thought required. Inspector Combridge, since he had heard the numbers of those notes, had become impatient to go. But an idea from Mr. Jellipot was not lightly to be refused. He sat back on the chair from which he had been about to rise.

"You are sure that I do not bore you? Very well. You will recall that in the Razor Street case there were three people who had been at the office of the dead man, and among whom the murderer was almost certainly to be found. Your difficulty there—apart from the fact that all the three would have had sufficient motive for the crime, which is hardly the case here—was that you could not exclude the possibility, however remote, that some other person had entered between their calls, and hurriedly committed the crime."

"Yes. We've got just the same trouble here."

"I think not. Or, at least, not if you accept the evidence of the man Glover in Bilton Terrace. There are possible intervals between the time when Forbes left and Bob Longworthy's call, between Mrs. Renshaw leaving and the time when Duckworth says he couldn't make anyone hear, even between Bob Longworthy's going and his mother's appearance on the scene, during which a man might have entered, hurriedly committed the crime, and fled. But the crime doesn't seem to have been committed in haste. The man who found time to take the bayonet out into the yard and give it a thorough wash, and then put it back in its place, wasn't in any hurry to get away. He was more concerned in removing evidences of how the murder had been committed, though even the reason for how he did that isn't easy to see."

"Yes. It's a funny business about washing the bayonet. But Glover says that it was done by a small man, which might mean either Longworthy or Duckworth, and now it seems that there won't be much more trouble in deciding between them. The man's given himself away, as they most often do."

Mr. Jellipot did not dispute this. He asked: "What do you propose to do now?"

"I am going to have a few words with Miss Lee, if I can find her at the shop. If possible, before she hears anything from the other two. I shall ask to have a look at the note which he's supposed to have given to her. I may find that it's more than one."

Mr. Jellipot considered this course of action, and had no criticism to offer.

"Yes," he said thoughtfully, "I don't think you could do anything better than that."

CHAPTER XVII.

SOME NEW FACTS FROM JESSICA LEE

THE stationery business for which Miss Lee had transferred her inheritance—with a considerable additional sum from her stepmother's bank account—to Henry Coldwater's pocket was situated in a busy by-street off Edgware Road, and still bore over its double front the trade name of F. C. Halters & Co., being that under which its difficult career had started.

Inspector Combridge, approaching it with alert and critical eyes, observed that it was on the wrong side of the street, and that it was entered by a rather steep step, which, as he had been correctly informed, is equivalent to asking for failure in a loud voice.

But he saw also that it had been newly painted, that the windows were brightly clean, and that the goods they showed were fresh, neatly ticketed and well displayed. He judged that the Lee-Renshaw-Longworthy family, perhaps materially aided by the astute counsels of the late Henry Coldwater, was making a hard fight against the natural destiny of the position in which the business had been established. But his own errand was not concerned with the financial fortunes of the stationery business. He entered the shop, waited while a neat assistant, blonde contrast to Jessica in appearance, but almost equally young, served two juvenile customers with a scribbling-pad and a box of sealing-wax of assorted colours, and then asked if Miss Lee were in.

"*Mrs. Lee*"—a slight inflexion corrected his style of designation—"is in. What name shall I say?"

"You can say that Chief Inspector Combridge would like to have a few words with her."

The girl's expression changed as she heard his name, causing him to wonder how much she might guess or know, but she only answered: "I'll see whether she's at liberty now," and within half a minute she was lifting up the flap of the counter, and inviting him into a small parlour behind the shop.

Jessica Lee rose to receive him from a table spread, not very tidily, with bread-and-butter and tea.

"You'll excuse the meal," she said. "I have tea rather early so that I can relieve Miss Rapp. But I thought, if you wanted to ask me anything about Mr. Coldwater, you might like to come in rather than talk in the shop."

He saw that there was a wedding-ring on her hand to support the fiction of "Mrs. Lee," and approved the wisdom of the attitude in which she accepted the result of her own folly and the baseness of an older man.

She looked to be in better spirits than when he had seen her first, and her manner was cool and self-controlled, as though his visit could have no troublesome reference to herself or those who were nearest to her; but her dark eyes, with their gipsy slant, flickered upon him, questioning, and not easy to read.

"Yes," he said, "we can talk better here. I saw Bob at midday, and told him—well, there's a question arisen about the numbers of some bank notes he had from Mr. Jellipot, and he told me he'd handed one or more to you."

He paused for a reply that did not come. Her face was expressionless now as she waited for him to go on.

"I thought you wouldn't mind letting me look at it for a moment."

"Do you mean that Bob may have been given a bad note?"

"No. The note is perfectly good. It's just the number I want to see."

"Why do you want that?"

The question was not either apprehensively or aggressively put. It was as though no more than natural curiosity uttered it, or even a politeness of sustaining the conversation, more neutral still. And the fact that she had not finished her meal reduced any significance there might be in the fact that she did not instantly rise to obtain the note Actually, as the inspector observed, she had not assented, unless by implication, to the suggestion that any such bank note was in her possession. In the most natural manner, she had only answered by questioning him.

But how should he answer now? A frank reply would be that he hoped it might be an essential link in a chain of evidence which would lead Bob Longworthy to the fatal noose. But that could not be bluntly said, and the faintest hint might transform the attitude of impersonal interest to one of hostility that would either lie or defy.

He wished he knew what her feelings were toward the dead man. Did she still persuade herself that she loved him, perhaps that he would have been induced to marry her, had he lived? Did she regard his murderer with gratitude or with bitter hate?

And what were her feelings towards those two, nominally mother and brother, who were actually no blood-relations of hers?

Superficial harmony there must certainly be. There might be something much more than that. It had been, unless he had been told much less than the truth, entirely on her behalf that both Bob Longworthy and his mother had called on the murdered man. Or, of course, the mother might have been actuated primarily or entirely by the desire to prevent any act of violence or folly on the part of her son, such as she had been too late to avert.

But, even so, it showed the "brother" at least as being devoted to Jessica to the point of murdering the man who had done her wrong! Would she be ungrateful for that? Even this question was not easy to answer. Women are not invariably pleased by such interventions. He saw he must be cautious in his reply, though he did not anticipate any serious difficulty in getting that for which he had come, and probably more. He played the game as fairly as its nature allowed, but her youth, her inexperience, the fact that she was emotionally as well as rationally concerned, made it a contest in which the dice were loaded against her.

He said: "It is a question of whether Mr. Jellipot gave him the right notes."

She looked puzzled at that. "I don't see," she said, "that that matters much. Not if they were the same amounts."

He saw that she was shrewder than he had supposed, but was still in doubt of whether she were fencing with him, or speaking with the ingenuousness that her manner indicated.

"Well," he said briefly, "it does. It's rather important that there shouldn't be any mistake."

She looked at him straightly, and her words were as direct as her eyes. "Of course, there's more in it than that. I'm not silly enough to suppose that that would have brought you here. But if you'll tell me what it really is that you want to know I expect I can put you right. I dare say it wasn't the same note at all, but there's no reason you shouldn't know."

Inspector Combridge saw that the time for frankness had come, which he no longer had cause to avoid, for he saw also that she had said too much to withdraw, even if she should regret it later. Perhaps, to her knowledge, not the same note at all? There must be pregnant meaning in that.

95

"The fact is," he said, "that Bob has paid away a note which he told me was one of two he had from Mr. Jellipot, and I know that isn't true, because the numbers of those notes are known, and they are not the same. There may be quite a simple and proper explanation, but at present all I know is that your brother has told me something that wasn't true, and it has become necessary to clear it up."

"Then there needn't be any trouble about that," she answered easily. "Bob gave me the notes he had from Mr. Jellipot. I didn't want to take them. I don't want to have more money from Bob or Mother. I want to pay back some of that which Mother couldn't afford to find. And I wasn't wanting it at the moment. But I couldn't say it mightn't be welcome when the rent and some accounts come due next month. Besides, I've got Miss Rapp's wages to think of now."

She checked herself abruptly, as the reason for that necessity came to her mind, concerning which she did not know how much, if anything, the inspector knew, and then went on hurriedly:

"But when I took it, I thought he was keeping the balance—the five pounds. When I heard that he was meaning to give Mother that to make up the rent, I made him take back one of the notes, and in the end he got it changed, and gave me seven pounds and kept three for himself.

"You see, he's only earning thirty-five shillings a week, and he's been giving Mother thirty-two-and-sixpence of that since we've been short, so I knew how he must be. I tried to get him to take more than that."

Inspector Combridge had listened patiently to this somewhat prolix explanation, which yet did not give the vital information he sought. He wanted the girl to talk as freely and as much as she would. But when he saw that she appeared to consider that she had given him a sufficient answer, he said: "Yes, I've no doubt that's how it was. In fact, your brother had told me about you making him keep the three pounds already, and I know how he got the note changed, but you haven't told me how it could be of a different number."

"Oh, no. I forgot that. But it's quite easy to guess. I'd got a few other notes, and I must have given him back a different one from those that he gave me. But I can't see that that matters to you."

"Perhaps not. But perhaps it may, all the same. Or perhaps it won't if you'll just tell me how the note that you did give him came into your hands."

For the first time the girl showed open resentment at the inquisition to which she was subject, though it was without evidence either of alarm or confusion.

"I don't see," she said, "that there's any need for me to answer that. I don't see that what I do with my own money's anything to do with the police."

"I am not suggesting that you have done anything wrong. But the bank note that you gave to Bob was one that it had become my duty to trace. All I am asking is how and when it came into your hands."

The girl became silent. She looked anxious, troubled. Inspector Combridge waited patiently. If she were inventing a lie which could be disproved, if she were about to say that that note was given to her at some time before it was paid to Mrs. Forbes, he might find that full confession of what she knew would soon be obtainable from a badly frightened girl.

"Well," she said at last, "I still don't see what it's got to do with you. But I don't see why you shouldn't know. I don't know whether Mother told you that we all thought that I'd paid a lot too much for the shop?"

"Yes. She told me that."

"Well, that's why it was. Mr. Coldwater came here on the—on the day he was killed, and gave me fifty pounds back. It was part of that."

"Fifty pounds in notes?"

"Yes. Ten-pound notes."

"About what time did he come?"

"About dinner-time."

"You mean at midday?"

"Yes. About then."

"Of course, you gave him a receipt?"

"No."

"Surely he asked for one?"

"No. I don't see why he should."

"Wouldn't it have been a natural thing for you to do?"

"Well, I didn't, anyway. I should if he'd asked. He wasn't here very long."

"You've still got the other four notes?"

"Yes. "

"You wouldn't mind me seeing them?"

"Yes. I think I should."

"Why?"

"I don't show anyone where I keep the money. We're only two girls in the shop."

"You don't really think I should steal your money?"

"You wouldn't steal it. You might make some excuse for not giving it back. It would come to about the same thing."

"You're not intending to pay those notes away?"

"Not till after the end of the month. I wouldn't promise longer than that."

"You'll let me look at them if I assure you that I will hand them back to you?"

"I think I'd rather talk it over with Mother before I do anything more. I expect I've said a lot now that I'd better not. I don't see what it's to do with me how Mr. Coldwater got killed."

"You wouldn't mind helping us to find out who murdered him?"

The answer came without either enthusiasm or reluctance: "No, I don't see why I should mind that."

"Then could you tell me something on a quite different matter. When Mr. Coldwater called here that day, did you notice whether he were carrying a parcel—a rather heavy parcel—and if so, could you tell me whether he said anything about where he'd got it from, or what it contained?"

"No. I dare say he had. I didn't notice particularly."

It was a natural answer, but, as it was given, the girl's voice had become guarded, her eyes fell. He could not decide whether it were the reticence of knowledge she did not wish to disclose, or merely the result of a determination not to be drawn into further confidences of any kind.

"No. You wouldn't be likely to have noticed particularly. But it would have been a heavy parcel. He would have laid it down while he talked."

"He didn't mention it, anyhow. We were talking about other things."

"In the shop, or did he come in here?"

"He wasn't likely to have given me that money in the shop."

"How long was he here?"

"I didn't notice particularly. Not so long."

"Half an hour?"

"I shouldn't think it was that."

"Did he have his lunch here?"

"No, of course not. It would have been rather queer if he had!"

The resentment in her voice had become evident again. That she was telling the truth might be doubted, but so also might be the object with which she lied. If she supposed him to be ignorant of her relations with Coldwater, if she wished to be the "Mrs. Lee" to him which was her probable pose to the assistant she had engaged against the time when she would no longer be able to serve, she might naturally avoid admissions which would disclose any kind of intimate familiarity between herself and the murdered man.

And on the vital point to which his enquiry had been directed she had given an explanation which, if it were true, relieved Bob Longworthy from any further difficulty in accounting for how he came to be in possession of the note. It was an explanation satisfactory in itself, but, to the inspector, it held no satisfaction at all. His patient pertinacity had cleared up the question of what had become of the notes which Mrs. Forbes had paid to the murdered man. He had obtained a little further information concerning his movements during the two midday hours in which he might have been absent from Coldwater House. But the explanation, the information, threw no light whatever upon the problem he had to solve. Or, if it did, it was to no further extent than that it confirmed the narrative which Mrs. Forbes had given. It finally removed what had never been more than a baseless suspicion that Basil Forbes might have recovered, and perhaps afterwards destroyed, the notes which had been the property of his wife.

So far as it made any difference at all, it caused suspicion to settle more definitely upon Bob Longworthy and Thomas Duckworth; and the fact that Bob's possession of the wrong note had been cleared up seemed to weight the scale further against the butler, whose character was, in other respects, of so tarnished a quality.

He asked himself, was he stalemated again? Or what more was there to do? There was the probability that Jessica could tell him more than she had: the faint possibility that it might contain something useful for him to know. It was through Mrs. Renshaw, if at all, that she could be persuaded to further speech. Mrs. Renshaw could not be expected to assist him in building up a case against her own son, but she might not regard the matter in that—she might regard it in an opposite—light.

Seeing no other opening through which advance could be made, he determined to interview Mrs. Renshaw again, and solicit her help with a frank admission of his dilemma. The question of her son's guilt or innocence could not be a matter on which she was likely to be in doubt. If she had seen Coldwater alive after Bob had left, as she most circumstantially asserted, she might be the only person, except Bob himself and the actual murderer, who knew him to be innocent with an absolute certainty. Determining to see Mrs.

Renshaw before her step-daughter would have returned home, and having walked some distance along Edgware Road while this resolution formed in his mind, he now boarded a No. 15 bus, dropped off in Bayswater Road, and arrived at Amptill Terrace in time to find Mrs. Renshaw about to commence a better-served tea than the premature meal which he had interrupted on F. C. Halters & Co.'s premises, and to be invited, with a quiet hospitality, to sit down to share it.

CHAPTER XVIII.

MRS. RENSHAW HAS MORE TO SAY

CHIEF INSPECTOR COMBRIDGE fulfilled the programme of frankness on which he had resolved. He narrated in sufficient detail the history of the bank notes, and the substance of the conversations he had had with Bob and Jessica during the day. He omitted only to mention that Henry Coldwater had received the money from Mrs. Forbes, recognising that her business had been of a private nature, and confined himself to stating the crucial fact that it had been paid to Coldwater only on the morning on which he died.

He mentioned also, with a similar reticence of description, the heavy and valuable parcel which the murdered man had probably collected during his midday absence from Coldwater House, and which might have, he implied, some connection with the crime. Was it not possible that Jessica, who had, on her own admission, been talking to him within two or three hours of his death, might know more of his movements during that luncheon hour—perhaps other circumstances bearing even more directly upon the crime—than she had been disposed to tell?

Mrs. Renshaw proved to be a good listener, attending closely, and interrupting seldom. When he finished, she said: "You'd have spared yourself some trouble if you'd understood that Bob wouldn't tell lies." She dismissed the possibility with a quiet smiling finality, giving him a sense not so much of having been rebuked as told, with entire politeness, that his capacity for judging his fellow men might be more than it was without being overmuch.

He countered shrewdly with the question: "But you wouldn't ask me to judge Miss Lee quite in the same way?"

She avoided an immediate reply by correcting him: "I ought to have told you, we agreed to call her Mrs. Lee now. We say her husband's abroad. Her name having been different from mine, they accepted the correction quite naturally here. Miss Williams apologised for not having understood at first. The girl at the shop, Miss Rapp, has never heard her called anything else."

"I'm sorry," he said, "that I didn't know before. I'll be careful now."

"It saves needless explanations. As to Jessica, I see what you mean. Of course, she's quite different. She's no blood relation at all, as I think I've told you. But I should call her a naturally truthful girl. And I don't think she gave you any reason to complain. She seems to have told you a good deal, and I should say it was quite accurate, though it wasn't what you were hoping to hear."

"But she might have told me a bit more?"

"Well, of course. But about what?"

"Say about the parcel that I'm almost sure Coldwater had, unless he picked it up somewhere after he left the shop."

Mrs. Renshaw did not respond instantly. Tea being over now, she had picked up some sewing on which her attention appeared to be concentrated. After a long pause she said: "Jessica ought to be here in about forty minutes. You can wait if you like. I think she'll take my advice. If she does, she'll tell you anything that she can, though I'm not suggesting that it will be any use."

"I'll take the chance of that," he said, settling down for a forty-minute wait in the comfortable chair to which she had guided him when the meal was over. "I've got to get something somewhere. I can't be worse off than I am now."

"Yes. I can understand how you feel." She went on for the next half-hour with a. flood of reminiscent anecdotes concerning Bob in his earlier years, and introducing his father's probity of word and conduct. He could not regard the picture she drew as inconsistent with his own observations, but he reminded himself that it was a mother who spoke, concerning a son who was not clear from suspicion of homicidal crime.

And was the character she drew as inconsistent wit such a deed as she would have liked him to think?

The iron-hard divisions of right and wrong that allowed no latitude either to compromise or condone, the religion that drew much of its vitality from the older scriptures that the Founder of Christianity had so sharply condemned, to what extremity might they not stir a mind that was young, emotional, rigid in its intellectual narrowness, and with its hatred of sinner and sin generously confused with sympathy for the companion of his childhood who had been betrayed in a shameful way?

While his mother's voice went placidly on, Inspector Combridge tried to visualise what might have occurred. It was not necessary to think that Bob had gone to Coldwater House with any murderous intention. He might have said no less than the truth when he told Superintendent Davis that he had gone to appeal to the "better nature" of Henry Coldwater. He had gone to appeal to him to marry Jessica, in what must have appeared to the older and utterly unscrupulous man an absurd and canting phraseology, at which he would be likely, indeed almost certain, to sneer. And then Bob Longworthy had struck him with the deadly weapon so near at hand in what he would tell himself had been a passion of righteous wrath! Looked at thus, it became at least a possible thing.

And the washing of the bayonet? It might not seem a very sane thing for him—but then it was not a sane thing for *any* man to have done! And it was somewhat less impossible as the act of a stupid boy—and Bob's wits did not appear to be very bright—half-stunned by the sudden horror of the deed, than as that of an older, more astute, or more deliberate criminal.

It was possible to imagine it being done by him as an act of mere stupidity, but substitute Thomas Duckworth, and it became crudely incredible, unless there were some explanation of policy or compulsion such as imagination failed to suggest.

Yes, he would certainly want to hear anything that Jessica might be willing to say. But that, he reminded himself, would be more likely to give him light on the transaction with Duckworth's illicit pledge. What a nightmare the case was!

"I think," Mrs. Renshaw said, "that Jessica is at the door now."

CHAPTER XIX.

Concerning a Back Room

JESSICA entered the room with an animation which may have had its origin in some eagerness to tell Mrs. Renshaw of the inspector's visit that afternoon. She began: "Oh, Mother, I've had—" and then stopped abruptly as she saw that they were not alone. Her brows drew to a frown. She stood taking off her hat, as though uncertain whether to advance or retire. She addressed Inspector Combridge with no friendliness in her voice: "I expect you've told Mother that you saw me this afternoon."

Mrs. Renshaw took quiet control of the situation. "Jessica," she said, "I have explained matters thoroughly to Inspector Combridge. I thought it was the best way. But I haven't mentioned the back room. I think you'd better tell him about that, and he'll understand we've given him all the help that we can."

It was a remark which left the girl little option of reticence regarding "the back room," whatever revelations it might involve, but she appeared to accept the position readily. She advanced into the room, the shadow clearing from her face, and the sharpness leaving her voice, as she said: "Oh, well, Mother, of course, if you think it's best! But," her eyes turning to Inspector Combridge, "I don't want anything public that mixes me up with Henry. I don't mind anything except that." Her glance turned back to her mother as she added, as though in an explanation she would understand: "Charlie was in again this morning. That's the third time this week."

"If we find we're treated with confidence," Inspector Combridge replied, "we always do our best to prevent any trouble that isn't necessary."

"Well," she said, "there's not much to tell, after all. When we made a fuss about the takings being less than half what we'd been told, Henry—Mr. Coldwater, I mean—said he'd help me by renting the big room at the back. There's the little room you came into, where we have meals, and behind it—the premises go rather far back—there's a room we use as a store. But on the other side—you remember it's a double-fronted shop—there was just one big room that went all the way back. There's an entrance up from Pritchett Street for delivering goods, and that was the way Henry always used to come.

"He said he could use the room for storage, and would pay me a pound a week, but he didn't want it talked about, because it might make a difference to how he got taxed, and if it was he should give it up. So of course I didn't. Even Mother didn't know about it, at first, and not until all the trouble began.

"He didn't only use it for storage. He put up a partition, and had half of it fitted up as a living-room, where he could stay the night if he wanted to be alone, as he said he did now and then. The other half was full of all sorts of things, on a lot of shelves that he had put up, and there is a safe that I never even saw him open or shut. Mr. Flipp has cleared it out now."

Inspector Combridge interrupted sharply: "You mean Flipp's been there since the murder?"

"Yes, he came next day, and took a lot of things away that he said belonged to Mr. Coldwater's customers. I supposed it was all right, as he'd been there before, and he had the key."

"Yes. That was quite natural. Go on." He resolved not to interrupt again. Let the girl tell her tale first in her own way! Its main outlines were clear enough already, beyond what she was likely to put into words: the cunning way in which Coldwater had used the occasion, when he found that she was there practically alone during the day, and perhaps for an hour more or less after the shop was closed, to provide at once a place where he could hide anything dishonestly acquired, a refuge if any sudden trouble with the law should make it prudent to lie low, and an opportunity for seducing a young and attractive girl. Inspector Combridge confirmed a previous suspicion that whoever had pushed that bayonet under his ribs might have put it to a worse use, but it was an aspect of the matter with which he was not officially concerned. He had only to find who that person was, and the moral and legal issues were for the determination of higher powers.

Jessica went on: "Well, he used to come a good deal, always using the Pritchett Street passage, so that he was never seen in the shop, and he told me more than once, and again that morning when he gave me the fifty pounds, that if anything happened to him all the stuff that he'd got there would be mine. He said no one else except I even knew it was there—"

"But you said that Flipp—"

"Except Mr. Flipp. But he hadn't meant that he should. I know that, because the first time he came there was a dreadful row. At least, it was all on one side. Henry cursed him, and asked how he'd found his way there, and Mr. Flipp just smiled and said he was sorry, but he hadn't supposed there was any secret about it. It wasn't what you'd call a nice smile. And after that he came bringing things, or on messages, several times."

"What we have been wondering." Mrs. Renshaw interposed, as Jessica's narrative paused for a moment, "is whether those things are legally hers."

"It's hardly my business to advise you on that," Inspector Combridge answered. "What sort of things are there?"

"There's furniture—some of it quite valuable—in the one room—I mean one side of the partition—and a lot of mixed stuff at the back. There are quite a lot of heavy parcels with nothing to indicate what they contain. I've told Jessica to leave everything as it was, and wait to see what happens. But as I've told you everything else, I thought it best that you should know that."

"I should think it was good advice. We haven't come on a will, nor been able to trace any relatives yet, so it looks like what he left going to the State more likely than not.

"I'll have a look round myself in the morning, but if there's nothing criminal about it, it won't be our business to interfere. If he gave it to you, I should say you've got a better claim than anyone else; but you ought to see your own lawyer about that. It's out of my line. I suppose"—he had turned to Jessica as he made this reply—"you can't tell me any more about that parcel I spoke of this afternoon?"

"No, I can't; beyond this. He certainly didn't bring one in with him, nor have it with him when he was talking to me. But he went into his own room for a few minutes before he left, and I believe there was something under his arm after that."

There being no more to be told, Inspector Combridge rose to go, but, as Jessica withdrew to her own room, he lingered a moment to thank the older woman for the information he had been given. "I don't quite see," he added, "what use it's likely to be—but you never know!" And then, as an after-thought: "I suppose the Charlie Miss—Mrs.—Lee mentioned doesn't come into the picture at all?"

"Only so far that he is a young man who wanted to marry her, and she turned him down. She said he was too stodgy for her. And now that Coldwater's dead, he's making it as plain as he can that he hasn't altered his mind, and I think he'll marry her at once if she'll agree, in spite of everything. She will, if she listens to me. It would be best in more ways than one."

"He's not the sort who might think it worth while to put Coldwater out of the way?"

Mrs. Renshaw allowed herself one of her rare smiles.

"He wouldn't have killed him, if you mean that. Not in business hours, anyway. Charlie Brice takes his own life far too seriously for that. He's in charge of the experimental laboratories of Hart & Peasley, the wholesale chemists, and I believe they say he hasn't been thirty seconds late since he was apprenticed ten or more years ago."

Inspector Combridge shook hands and went. He did not think that Charlie Brice was likely to solve the problem that vexed his mind, though he resolved to enquire whether he had been at business as usual on the afternoon of the crime. He saw that a man of his occupation would be more likely to give an enemy something to swallow than poke him up with a bayonet. But he found that he had a good deal of other matter on which to think.

As to those back rooms, the use of which, apart from Mrs. Renshaw's candour, he might never have been led to suspect, they might have no connexion with the crime, but it would be interesting to look them over tomorrow. If they should prove to be of no importance to him, he thought, and was inclined to hope, that the girl would be left in undisturbed possession of whatever they might contain. The position was not unlike that of a woman who is given a flat and its contents by a man whose mistress she becomes. And as he had promised her marriage, she deserved rather more consideration than—but that was not his matter at all.

He had little doubt that that back room had been the hiding-place for Viscount Swinfield's plate, and that one of the purposes of Coldwater's call had been to collect it in readiness to hand it over to Duckworth that afternoon. But, if so, it was evident that he was intending to keep faith with the anxious butler, and there was no more motive for Duckworth to have murdered him than evidence that he had.

But he would have a few words to say to Theophilus Flipp. It was evident that his frankness had been limited by what he thought would be discovered in other ways. And what had he received from his employer's safe on the morning after the crime? How had he obtained the key? His tale about the safe at Coldwater House might be true. It sounded probable. He might have had a key to that. But that he had legitimate access to Coldwater's safe at his secret lair was made improbable by the quarrel of which Jessica had spoken.

Probably Flipp hoped now that no one would ever know of the use to which that back room had been put, or of its content, except Jessica and himself, and he might be intending to blackmail her for some part of what would be realised from them. Perhaps it would be better not to challenge him on these matters, but to have his movements watched, by which other unsuspected things might be disclosed.

For the first time, Inspector Combridge considered him seriously as a potential murderer. Who could tell what friction there might have been between the master-criminal and the assistant whose position was confidential, but not really trusted, as Coldwater's anger when his retreat was discovered had clearly shown? Who could guess what impulse of fear or greed might have urged him to plan the crime?

He was a man—the one man—who could get access to Henry Coldwater at any time, and who could strike when he would be off his guard. But, though he was not conspicuously tall, he could not be described accurately as a short man, and why, in heaven's name, if he had committed the murder, should he have washed the bayonet in the yard? He was a man who must have been known by sight, who might have been recognised from any of a dozen neighbouring windows. For a stranger to do that—as it seemed that some stranger had!—seemed an incredible lunacy, but for him—well, it was not an idea that could be seriously entertained.

Inspector Combridge's mind reverting to the subject of the gold plate, he had a fresh doubt. He had only Flipp's word for the fact that he had found it on the morning after the murder in the safe at Coldwater House. Suppose that it was that which he had fetched from the safe behind Jessica's shop? If so, as he did not wish to reveal the existence of that resort, it was a lie he would have been almost certain to tell. So the theory of Coldwater acting, in good faith to the butler was based on no more than Flipp's word, under circumstances which, if it were not true, would have almost impelled him to lie!

From this confusion of doubt, his mind went on to a quite different speculation. The notes that had been in the possession of Mrs. Forbes in the morning had passed into that of Jessica Lee in the afternoon. That was clear. She said they had been given to her. That might be, but there was no proof. Nothing but her own assertion.

Suppose that she had returned with Coldwater to his office, quarrelled with him, and killed him there, and taken the notes which might have been lying temptingly on his desk? That was possible, except for the fact that Basil Forbes had thrashed him in the afternoon. But why should she not have been on the premises at the time—perhaps have overheard from an adjoining room, and been filled with contempt and loathing of the man who had seduced her, whose base blackmailing operations had been exposed to her ears, and who had been beaten so ignominiously?

It was possible—barely possible—though he did not think the crime to have been a woman's work, and there was always that figure in the yard. And it was not his business to formulate possibilities. Any fool can do that. It was his business to find the proofs. What a nightmare, he said to himself again—what a nightmare the whole thing was!

CHAPTER XX.

MRS. RENSHAW SEES MR. JELLIPOT

IT was three weeks later than Richard Dyke entered Mr Jellipot's office to announce that a Mrs. Renshaw had called to see him on business the nature of which she declined to state. Mr. Jellipot, who thought he knew what it would be—on which his guess was only partially right—sighed, and said: "Well, show the lady in."

Mrs. Renshaw came in, looking her usual quiet and controlled self, though with signs of worry that might have been observed by a critical eye, and gave the solicitor occasion for immediate approbation by the prompt and explicit manner in which she stated the objects of her call.

"I want to ask you," she said, "to advise me respecting my stepdaughter's claim upon property which Henry Coldwater left on her premises, and I should also like to have an understanding with you that you will undertake the defence of my son Robert, if he should be accused of Coldwater's murder, which I think probable."

Mr. Jellipot temporised: "I don't think I have acted for you previously. Perhaps you wouldn't mind telling me who recommended you to me?"

"I thought I could not do better than come to you, as you know so much of the case already, and it was through that reward you offered that Bob first got into touch with the police."

"Which you would rather he hadn't done?"

"I thought it foolish. But so far as the matter of clearing Mr. Forbes of suspicion was concerned, I wouldn't say that it was more than his duty to have come forward."

"I wonder whether you have considered, Mrs. Renshaw, that I can't blow hot and cold. I went to some trouble and expense on behalf of Mr. Forbes to show that he was an innocent man, and your son's visit to the murdered man took place almost immediately after he left. Don't you think it might be better to go to someone who

110

could handle the case with more freedom than I might feel able to do?"

"I don't think any difficulty would arise over that. I shouldn't wish you to suggest that Mr. Forbes killed him. Both Bob and I know the contrary. We know that he was alive in the afternoon."

Mr. Jellipot became thoughtful. He asked: "Suppose your son were advised to plead guilty? I can imagine a reconstruction of the event by which a certain amount of public sympathy would be stirred."

Mrs. Renshaw put this suggestion aside. "There is no question of that," she said. "Bob is absolutely innocent. I saw the man alive myself after he left." But Mr. Jellipot observed that she had not been roused to any indignation of protest by his readiness to suggest that her son was guilty. She simply indicated that his defence would be of an opposite kind.

"There is no need to decide the matter this afternoon? At present, your son is not even under arrest?"

"No. But I think that is what Inspector Combridge is meaning to do."

Mr. Jellipot did not dispute this. He had reason for thinking that Mrs. Renshaw had guessed correctly what was about to happen. He answered: "Well, it is a matter to which I must give some consideration. I don't like criminal cases. Suppose I give you an answer this time tomorrow?"

Mrs. Renshaw did not look pleased, but she accepted the position readily. "Very well," she said, "we must leave it till then. But I shall hope that you won't refuse."

"And now," he said, more genially than he had spoken before, "suppose you tell me your other troubles."

He settled himself to listen quietly to a tale much of which, from another angle, he already knew.

Henry Coldwater, when alive, had been suspected of many delinquencies, but they had not guessed that his main occupation had been that of a receiver of stolen goods. Indeed, they saw reason now to suspect that they had been doubly fooled. They had watched him acting as a business transfer agent on the frequent verge of criminality; they had had hints of his blackmailing activities, though without ever being able to obtain material for a prosecution, and they were now reduced to wonder whether some at least of these dubious transactions might not have been deliberately staged to draw their attention away from his more constant occupation. Some ostensible occupation it had been necessary for him to have, and in that of a business transfer agent he had approached respectability as nearly as it was his nature to do.

It was less than three months before that the C.I.D. had received an anonymous hint that the cellars of a firm of wholesale jewellers of hitherto unblemished reputation would be found to be a harbour for stolen goods, and, with some hesitation, a search warrant had been obtained and the place raided, with no result.

It was a bitter memory, and the claim for compensation from the outraged jewellers had still been vexing the Chiefs of the C.I.D., loath alike to make financial confession of error or to face the publicity which was the threatened alternative, when Inspector Combridge, considerately avoiding the front entrance of F. C. Halters & Co.'s premises, had walked up the Pritchett Street passage into a room which, within half an hour, had revealed the proceeds of some of the most successful burglaries of the last three years, and conclusive evidence that one at least of the cases of stolen goods had had a previous location in the cellar that had been unsuccessfully raided three months before.

It had been a spectacular triumph for Inspector Combridge, causing even the question of the missing murderer to be momentarily forgotten, and his own feelings had not been without gratitude to the two women whose frankness had put him upon the scent. But, gradually, the official view had changed.

There might be no cause for suspicion against—there might even be occasion for legitimate gratitude towards—the older woman; but was it equally certain that Jessica Lee, the admitted mistress of the dead man, had been clear of guilty knowledge when she had provided that secret harbourage for the stolen goods?

The fact that the bank notes which were the profit of the successful blackmailing of Alice Forbes had passed so promptly into her custody was capable of a very different interpretation from that which she had put forward, and though there might be insufficient evidence to justify her appearance in the dock beside Theophilus Flipp, whose well-paid lawyers were now struggling desperately to provide that gentleman with a defence which might survive the summing-up of any competent judge, yet there was no disposition to consider favourably the rather hesitant claims that "Mrs." Lee had made to such furniture and other effects as could not be shown to be stolen property.

Faced with this position, she would probably have resigned her claim without protest, and Mrs. Renshaw, now acutely concerned for the safety of her threatened son, might have been content to see the police have their wills on this minor issue, but Mr. Charles

Brice, now speaking with the authority of a husband-to-be, had protested against their attitude with unexpected vigour.

He had avoided any expression of opinion as to the guilt or innocence of Bob Longworthy, but he had no hesitation in regarding his fiancée as a deluded victim, and, that being so, he had argued that her proper course was to assert her rights with the greater emphasis for the aspersion that was cast upon her.

"I don't care much about the stuff," he said. "If Coldwater had left you a fortune, I might have thought it was too dirty to touch. And as to having any of his furniture in a house of ours—I'd rather set fire to it with my own hands. But if the things are legally yours, and you stand by while the police take them away, they'll think you're afraid because you've been mixed up with a crook, and that's just the reason you ought to act differently."

Mrs. Renshaw, hearing this opinion repeated by Jessica (who was divided between inclination to avoid further trouble, anxiety not to act in a manner which might diminish Charlie Brice's opinion of her courage, or confidence in her innocence, and unwillingness to cause her stepmother distress), had said that it was a matter on which she ought not to act without legal advice, and offered to see Mr. Jellipot on her behalf, to which Jessica had readily agreed.

The point was of the kind which were the favourite recreation of Mr. Jellipot's legal mind. After closely questioning Mrs. Renshaw upon the circumstances of Henry Coldwater's partial occupation of the premises, and the introduction of his effects upon them, he wrote out a list of questions to which he wished to have Jessica's written replies.

"In the meantime," he said, "I shall do no more than notify the police that, while we consent to the removal of any goods to which third parties may have been able to establish a valid claim, they must act at their own risk if they go beyond that, and under formal protest from us.

"But there is one point which I must make clear, although I do not go so far as to say that it should control, or even influence, our decision, which should rather be ruled by the facts, as disclosed by Miss Lee's replies. If we establish that a legal subtenancy had been created, then we go far to invalidate her claim upon these goods, which cannot be said to have been in her possession—except so far as we might be able to set up that she had been domiciled by her own tenant—when Coldwater was killed; while, on the other hand, if we succeed in establishing that there was no subtenancy, then Miss Lee must appreciate that it was upon her own premises that the admittedly stolen goods were found, and her responsibility for being in actual legal possession of them may be substantially increased thereby."

"But it was she who gave information about Mr. Coldwater having property there."

"Yes. That is a strong point in her favour, but not one that strengthens our present claim. May I ask when the marriage is to take place?"

"I believe they mean to have it next week."

"And I am sure that Miss Lee will make an excellent wife. I should like, if I may be allowed, to send my congratulations to both of them. I am sure, from the way he is acting in this matter, Mr. Brice is a gentleman whom it would be a pleasure to know."

Mrs. Renshaw said she would convey the message. She understood that, in giving this blessing to the projected union, Mr. Jellipot had implied his own judgment that Jessica had not been willingly involved in Henry Coldwater's criminal courses. It emboldened her to say, as she rose to leave: "Then I am to look in again tomorrow to hear your decision about Bob? I feel sure that you won't refuse to do what you can for an innocent boy."

Mr. Jellipot avoided a direct reply. He said: "I suppose it is the result of the identification parade that makes you feel sure that he will be charged?"

Mrs. Renshaw looked surprised. "I didn't suppose," she answered, "that you would have heard about that. It was what I was going to tell you, if you said you would take up the case. I don't think it was fairly done."

"Inspector Combridge was talking the case over with me last week. I understood that he was intending to invite your son to submit himself to such a test, but he must have told him that he had the right to refuse. Perhaps he ought to have taken legal advice at that time.

"I should tell you that I also heard what happened. But why do you think that test was unfair? Inspector Combridge is usually very careful in such matters."

"Well, for one thing, the men were all about the same height."

"You object to that? Might it not have been more unfair if the others had been taller than Bob? It is a difficult point."

"He understood that he had the right to refuse, but I thought it would look bad, and there couldn't be any risk, as we knew that he wasn't the one that Mr. Glover saw. But I suppose I was wrong."

Mr. Jellipot said vaguely that that didn't necessarily follow. He shook hands, and led her towards the door, without giving any further assurance as to what his decision would be.

114

CHAPTER XXI.

The Hesitation of Mr. Jellipot

MR JELLIPOT found real difficulty, during the remainder of the business day, in concentrating upon the various matters which came before him. The question of whether he should defend Mrs. Renshaw's "innocent boy" must be settled before tomorrow noon, and he had seldom been faced by a problem of equal difficulty.

It was not that he doubted his ability to conduct the defence to a successful issue. He did not think that Bob Longworthy would ever be convicted of murder, and he felt certain that he would not be hanged. Neither was his mind largely occupied by his own reluctance to undertake criminal business, or any concern for Inspector Combridge's probable chagrin if he should learn that they were once again to be on opposite sides. His problem was the line of defence which, if he should undertake it, it would be right to adopt, and the probable sequel that it would have. And, alternatively, he could not avoid the question of what the issue would be likely to be if he should decline the case, and it should be entrusted to others.

He knew that suspicion had been darkening upon Bob Longworthy during the last fortnight. The position had been simplified by the Assistant Commissioner's reluctant admission that Basil Forbes might be an innocent man. But, if so, he had argued with more than his usual logic, it almost certainly followed that Bob Longworthy was not.

Anyhow, it lay between Longworthy and Duckworth, and it had become time for Inspector Combridge to make up his mind.

Inspector Combridge saw that, if the choice were no more, there was no doubt which it must be. There was no evidence whatever to contradict Thomas Duckworth's account of how he had turned away from a closed door; no motive that could be fastened upon him to give an air of probability to the crime. He might be a man of less than doubtful honesty, but even if that could be brought out at the trial, or merely as a matter for the consideration of the police, it was of no importance at all. Dishonesty and violence do not always, nor indeed commonly, go hand in hand. In respect of this issue, Thomas Duckworth's record was as good as it could possibly be.

As to that, Bob Longworthy was of an equal mildness; but in his case there was motive of an undeniable kind. His very object in making the call was of a nature which, if it were rebuffed, as it was likely to have been, might lead to physical assault, as the only satisfaction that would remain. And added to this there was now the vague suspicion that the girl whom Coldwater had seduced might have become involved with him in the secret criminalities from which most of his income derived. Had Bob Longworthy known of this? And how, if so, had his conscience, in its narrow rigidity, reacted? Had he persuaded himself that it was his duty to save her, even at the price of his own sin?

Inspector Combridge excused himself from the embarrassment of an immediate arrest by arguing that, though the case might be sufficiently strong, to justify application for a warrant, and to secure a remand it was less than certain that a committal would follow. It was extremely unlikely that the boy would attempt to bolt, and should he do so, he would be arrested at once, after having improved the case against himself by the folly of the act. But though deferring the arrest, the inspector now accepted the theory that he had committed the crime, and concentrated upon the difficult task of completing the case against him.

In this he was assisted beyond reasonable anticipation by an erratic improvement in the memory of William Glover, who had recalled an incidental circumstance by which he was able to fix the time at which he had looked out from his third-story window upon the bayonet-washer in the yard of Coldwater House as between 3:30 and 4:00 P.M., or certainly not much later than that. This went far towards lifting the last shadow of suspicion from Thomas Duckworth, for if he had called at 4:15 would it not have been nearer 4:30 before he would have committed, and be clearing up the evidences of, the crime? But, for the indictment of Robert Longworthy, it was a most opportune recollection.

Seeking to make further bricks in the absence of any evident straw, Inspector Combridge had conceived the idea of an identification parade. Did Mr. Glover think that he might identify, either by gait or clothes, the man he had only seen from above? Mr. Glover was not sure, but he was quite willing to try.

Fortified by this undertaking, the inspector had approached both the suspected men, with the proposal that they should submit themselves to parade with ten others, to ascertain whether Glover could identify either of them. It was, he pointed out, a course which innocent men had no reason to fear, and that those under a false suspicion should actually welcome, as providing opportunity for demonstrating how baseless it was.

This argument might not have been effectual had it not been backed by the alternative possibility of actual arrest, which Thomas Duckworth knew, even if it were technically no more than "detention" at the police headquarters for the limited period which present practice allows, could hardly be less than ruinous to himself, in view of the nature of his business relations with the dead man, and the official explanations which Viscount Swinfield would be likely to receive.

In the case of Bob Longworthy, who, as he became conscious that he was under the continual observation of the police, had developed a stubborn dumbness, frightened and yet defiant, it is unlikely that he would have been persuaded to line up at the police-station by any argument short of actual arrest that Inspector Combridge could urge, had not his mother given him such advice, and hers was a voice which it was not his habit to disregard.

After that, there had been no remaining difficulty except to settle upon a time when the two suspected men could be present together; for which Bob would not consent to leave his employment during the day, and Thomas had duties during the evening hours which he must not miss. He suggested Sunday afternoon. But it appeared that Bob had a Sunday school class, the obligation of which was greater than that of more mundane things. In the end, Saturday afternoon had been the accepted solution, and when the line-up occurred, William Glover, after a single stroll along the row of self-conscious men, had stopped before Bob Longworthy, and said: "That's the man, almost for sure. If it was one of these, I should say it's him."

"You think you could swear to him?" Superintendent Davis had asked hopefully.

"I said I was almost sure. I don't think I'd care to go much farther than that."

Superintendent Davis shrugged slightly. He knew he must not persuade, but there is so little difference in fact, so much in law, between being "willing to swear," and being "almost sure"! He saw it to be a case of "the little less, and what works away."

"But you're quite sure," he asked again, "that it wasn't any of the others, if it wasn't he?"

117

Mr. Glover agreed, but preferred his own grammar to that of Superintendent Davis. "It wasn't none of them," he said with emphasis, "if it wasn't him."

So the parade had had one definite result. It had let Duckworth out.

Mr. Jellipot considered these circumstances, as they had been narrated to him by Inspector Combridge, and asked himself, had Mrs. Renshaw had reason on her side when she had said that the line-up had not been fair?

He knew that, in the hands of some officers, whose fault may have no worse origin than excessive zeal to convict those whom they have good reason for regarding as society's foes, such parades could be made to serve their purpose in several ways.

But he did not regard Inspector Combridge as likely to err in such directions, and Mrs. Renshaw's particular complaint did not seem entirely reasonable. Perhaps she did not know that William Glover had already said that the man he had seen was of less than average height. Certainly, if Bob had been put among a row of taller men, the complaint would have had more weight

He knew also that there was an alternative method of identification which is liable to greater abuse. Suppose William Glover had been put to stand at a street-corner which Bob would be sure to pass, and asked if he could recognize him as he went by? He might have been pointed out to a doubtful man who knew what the police suggested and desired, without ever knowing that the inquisition had taken place. And some form of identification there must surely be. Are cases to be taken into court, and witnesses put into the box to say for the first time whether the prisoner is the man they saw, or against whom their complaint was made? But the question of how much weight should be given to such identifications in cases of disputed identity is a more difficult one.

Mr. Jellipot's mind went over the whole circumstances as they reflected suspicion upon Bob Longworthy, which he was able to do the more swiftly and thoroughly because he had given a great deal of previous thought to considering them in other and broader aspects, and he concluded that, with some good counsel briefed for the defence, a conviction would be very difficult to obtain. The case might be made very unpleasant both for Bob himself and Jessica Lee—even for Mrs. Renshaw if her assertion that she had seen Henry Coldwater alive should be skilfully challenged, but, beyond that unpleasantness, the acquittal seemed sure enough. Suspicion there might be. But not enough to obtain the conviction of a young man of good character on the capital charge. Unless, of course, he should make a fool of himself in the witness-box, which is a risk no skill in advocacy can always avoid.

This was if the matter should follow a normal course; and it was just that about which he was less than sure, from which doubt arose this persistent indecision as to what he would say to Mrs. Renshaw tomorrow.

And, of course, Inspector Combridge might have unearthed some further evidence of a damning kind. It was always a mistake to hold an adversary too lightly, especially if, more through good fortune than skill, you have been successful in overcoming him once or twice before. And as Mr. Jellipot's thoughts came to this point, Inspector Combridge was announced.

CHAPTER XXII.

The Revelations of Sneaky Dawes

MR. JELLIPOT looked at Inspector Combridge in mild surprise, for he was in a state of visible excitement, which was not his usual demeanour, even under circumstances which few men could sustain with a quiet mind. "I suppose," he said, "that it is concerning the Coldwater case that you have been kind enough to look in."

"Yes. I should say it is. I've got on to something today that Sir Reginald Crowe will be interested to hear."

"Anything that is of importance to Sir Reginald cannot be indifferent to me," Mr. Jellipot answered, "but as it's also to do with the Coldwater case I think I ought to tell you, before you say more, that Mrs. Renshaw was here this morning, asking me to act for her son, if you should prosecute him, as she feared that you may be proposing to do."

As he said this, Mr. Jellipot anticipated some expression of annoyance, if not of protest against his acceptance of that advocacy, but Inspector Combridge appeared either not to hear, or to disregard the warning he had received.

He answered with apparent irrelevance: "I've been talking to Sneaky Dawes."

"I thought," Mr. Jellipot answered, "that that gentleman was in retirement in one of His Majesty's jails."

"So he is. But good-conduct prisoners are allowed a limited diet of daily newspapers, and he read that Henry Coldwater was dead. When he saw that he asked for a heart-to-heart talk with me."

"I should have supposed that someone from the Home office—"

"So they did. I believe they're a bit sulky about it still. But Sneaky wouldn't give way, and he knew they wouldn't miss the chance, if he seemed willing to talk. When I saw him, he said he'd stuck out for me because we'd been pals before—you see I arrested

120

him both times that we've been able to run him in—and he believed that if I promised anything there'd be a chance that it would get done. Besides, he'd heard that I knew Crowe."

"Then may I conclude that he gave you information about the Goffe Collection?"

"Yes, and a bit more. He's let out that Coldwater was the biggest receiver in London—the one that we've known *must* exist, but haven't been able to trace. Not for the last eight years."

"It sounds rather difficult to believe."

"It shows what mugs we can be."

"You are sure that Mr. Dawes is not pulling your leg now?"

"No. It was too detailed for that, and it fits in."

"I don't understand why, if Coldwater was in such a large way of—business—as that, he should have troubled himself to blackmail Mrs. Forbes for a pound a week."

"Yes. It does seem odd. But Sneaky's tale is that he wasn't really after the money in such cases as that. He'd have been quite as well content if she hadn't been able to pay. In fact, when she got her legacy and took in the balance of the amount, it may have been the last thing he expected or wished to happen. That Monday seems to have been a bad day for him from the start!

"But Sneaky says that he would go to any amount of trouble to get women into his hands, and perhaps use them, in the end, in his own schemes, as we've seen that he did with Jessica Lee."

"Well, I've no doubt that you are right. But you were going to tell me something about the Goffe Collection?"

"I haven't any definite news about that yet. But we know that it passed into Coldwater's hands, and that's a start on the right road."

"Dawes could tell you no more than that?"

"He either can't, or he won't. He wants to know where he comes in. You can't blame him for that." Mr. Jellipot did not discuss the abstruse ethical problems latent in the last remark, though they were of a kind which it would have been his pleasure to pursue at a more leisurely time. He said: "I suppose you'd like me to put the question before Sir Reginald, and get a promise from him?"

"Yes."

"What do you think he wants?"

"He'll wriggle hard for some remission of sentence—I don't know how far Sir Reginald can influence that—and a substantial sum in cash when he comes out."

"That," Mr. Jellipot reflected, "could hardly be considered an anti-social act, for it is by no means easy to see how such a man can avoid being drawn into further crime on his release, if he be without funds, and his character gone."

Inspector Combridge differed. "I should say you're miles out," he replied, "if you think Sneaky's a poor man. He's about the cleverest large-scale thief that's given us headaches since I came into the C.I.D. And you can suppose that he didn't hand that collection over without picking up something substantial on account, though you can't expect that he'll tell us that! He'll have his investments safely hidden away—with the help of some lady friends, more likely than not."

Mr. Jellipot said that he had no doubt that Inspector Combridge was right, and gave instructions for the chairman of the London & Northern Bank to be rung up.

The Goffe Collection of foreign stamps—the most complete collection of Africans in the world—had been purchased by Sir Reginald Crowe about two years before, from the estate of a deceased Californian millionaire, and insured for £80,000 during its passage to England. Its disappearance while in transit by registered parcel post and the subsequent arrest of Sneaky Dawes and two minor confederates, had furnished the Press of that year with some particularly interesting—the journalists had quaintly styled it "sensational"—copy. The convictions which followed were officially considered to have been the culmination of one of the Yard's most spectacular triumphs. But the fact that the crime had been reconstructed from no more than a three-inch fragment of waterproof packing material, greatly though it might add to the prestige of Detective-Inspector Brecks, was, in the opinion of Sir Reginald Crowe, a very poor consolation for the fact that the proceeds of the robbery had not been recovered, in spite of the reward of £8,000 which the underwriters had offered.

"The fact is," he had said to Detective-Inspector Brecks, with his usual uncompromising bluntness, "if we bankers were to conduct our business on such cross-eyed lines, we should be in the bankruptcy court in six months, and you'd have us all in the dock for it, more likely than not. You'd say that such stupidity wasn't possible without criminal intent, even though you couldn't see what we thought we were pulling off."

"Well, sir," the officer had replied, with the resentment which the rebuke had naturally aroused subdued by the outward respect due to even the youngest of the chairmen of the great London banks, "we've put Sneaky Dawes where he won't do any more mischief for the next five or six years. You can't say that we haven't made property safer by doing that."

"You needn't kid yourself," was the blunt reply, worded after the manner of one who considered that his dignity should be able to take care of itself, "that you're doing anything half as useful as that. I should say it's the other way round.

"As long as it's possible to get away with eighty thousand pounds worth of loot, at the cost of five or six years in quod, you'll find plenty ready to fill the cells; but if you went about it the other way, and didn't care overmuch about catching the thief, so long as you recovered the stolen goods, you'd soon find that there weren't many thieves to catch, because you'd have knocked the profit out of the game."

"In a very large proportion of cases—" the indignant officer began.

"Yes. I know that. I'm only telling you that it isn't enough, or the game wouldn't go on. If you roped in only half the poor devils you do, and got back twice the loot you recover now, you'd find that most of that class of criminal would give up a profession that didn't pay, and go in for something else, even if he had to learn how to make income-tax returns. And the fact that you hadn't put him in jail would make it easier for him to do.

"I know that I'm safe to get the insurance money, but it's not that I want. I want the stamps. The underwriters are offering the usual ten percent reward, and I'm willing to do the same. There'll be sixteen thousand pounds for whoever puts us on the track of the Goffe Collection, and that's a sum that even a head crook doesn't pick up every day of the week."

"We'll advertise that, of course, sir. But you know, we're not allowed to take rewards ourselves."

"Yes, I know all about that. You're not allowed unless you're allowed. We'll deal with that if the time ever comes that it could make any difference to you, as I hope it may."

That conversation had taken place two years before. But the huge reward had remained unclaimed. The insurance money had been paid into Sir Reginald's account, and there the matter appeared to have found its end.

If any part of the collection had been put on the market (which experts in the trade were disinclined to believe), it had been too entirely broken up, and mixed with other specimens, for its origin to be even suspected. It was regarded as more probable that Sneaky Dawes had failed to dispose of it before his arrest, and that it remained in some hiding-place only known to himself and those who could not be tempted to betray his—and perhaps their own—interests even for the sum of £16,000.

123

But it now appeared that this theory had been wrong. If Sneaky Dawes' present statement were to be believed, the collection had passed intact into the hands of Henry Coldwater, who would have paid him a sum of no less than £20,000 when he should be free to receive it. But now that Coldwater was dead, from whom could Sneaky look for the reward of one of the cleverest thefts of the century, and for which he was undergoing so long a period of enforced retirement?

Alive, Henry Coldwater had had a reputation for keeping bargains with his customers, apart from which the cleverest of receivers will find little business coming in his direction; but, he being dead events might move to a different conclusion. It was improbable that he had left a properly executed will directing the payment of his just debts, and scheduling Egbert John (otherwise Sneaky) Dawes thereamong for an item of £20,000!

Mr. Dawes, considering these circumstances, had decided that he must do something for the protection of his own interests. He was not a squealer. But it is impossible to betray the dead to the vengeance of English law. He had given Inspector Combridge some surprising information. He had indicated that, if he could depend upon the honour and liberality of Sir Reginald Crowe as absolutely as he had been able to trust those admirable qualities in Henry Coldwater, he might have still more to say.

Now, with these circumstances, past and present, before his mind, Mr. Jellipot took up the telephone, and heard Sir Reginald's voice enquiring rather abruptly on what business he had felt it necessary to ring him up in what was known to be his busiest hour.

CHAPTER XXIII.

MR. JELLIPOT WILL NOT DECIDE

"YOU can tell Combridge," Sir Reginald's voice came crisply over the wire, when Mr. Jellipot had finished his own narration, "that the position is this: of course the underwriters' offer is still open. That's eight thousand pounds, and I needn't say that they'd be glad to shell out, because it would mean getting eighty thousand pounds back from me, or picking up a stamp collection that would be worth more than that. But how they'd stomach making any bargain with Dawes is more than I'd like to say. Aaronson is always a bit stuffy about going against the law, and whether he'd be doing that you're the best judge.

"But if I get that collection back in good condition—in *good condition, and every stamp in its place*—I'll promise to have Dawes out of quod within six months, if I have to unload on the market just as the Government's relying on us to dress it for the new loan, and then—but you'd better not tell Combridge that. Nor that Dawes wouldn't find his pocket empty when he gets free. Tell him to make the man understand that he won't be sorry. You can say the less I promise the more I do. You'll know how to put it to him. And I'll rely on you both to have that collection found in time for me to queer the pitch for that loan, if—but I've told you not to say anything about that."

"It is not a form of argument, as addressed to any member of His Majesty's Government," Mr. Jellipot replied seriously, "which I should under any circumstances advise. Nor is it one that I should use, even verbally, without the most explicit instructions from you; but if you will rely upon my discretion—"

At this point, there was an exclamation of "Good old Jellipot!" and the click of a disconnection at the other end of the wire.

Mr. Jellipot hung up the receiver. He said: "Sir Reginald has, I think, been interrupted by business of some urgency, but, before being disconnected, he had been good enough to give me an absolutely free hand in this matter, and you can feel confident that any verbal undertaking which you may find it expedient to give in Sir Reginald's name will be exactly similar to the voluntary action which Sir Reginald will take upon my advice when the collection has been recovered."

Inspector Combridge looked puzzled, and then smiled as he realised the nature and circumspection of this undertaking.

"Yes," he said, "coming from you and Crowe that ought to be good enough. Of course, you understand that it's not only the Goffe Collection we hope to spot. If Dawes has told us no more than the truth, Coldwater has got—or at least had—the proceeds of half a dozen big robberies of various kinds that we've never been able to trace. We've had several very interesting finds already, but it seems evident now that there is a more important depository than that up the Pritchett Street passage. We're on a bigger thing than we guessed, and now that Dawes has begun to talk he's got to be persuaded to go on, even if he gets half his sentence lopped off."

"But," Mr. Jellipot suggested, "the Home Office would prefer that the reward, the promises, don't come directly from them?"

Inspector Combridge did not deny that. He said: "Well, I've been straight with you. The Goffe Collection's about the biggest plum that we're likely to pick, and I knew Sir Reginald would rather have it than the cash. It isn't everyone who's been paid the insurance who wants to hear that the goods are back on the table again."

"No. Probably not. I suppose this new development doesn't suggest to your mind that there may be an explanation of the murder different from anything that we've had in mind, and that the question of arresting young Longworthy might be deferred?"

Inspector Combridge considered this, and then spoke with deliberation. "No, I can't see that it does. If the scent that we're on now bears on the murder at all, I should say it's more likely to show that he had some extra reason for what he did. You may find that that family is mixed up with Coldwater a lot more than we've been supposing."

"It is," Mr. Jellipot admitted, "a legitimate speculation."

"You mean you don't believe it at all?"

"It is not a point on which I am prepared to express an opinion. But do I understand that you are still disposed to make the arrest?"

"Yes. You can understand that."

"You realise that you will have one of the weakest cases that can ever have got a verdict of guilty from an English jury?"

"I'd answer that better if I'd seen Bob and his mother go into the box—as they'll have to do, or he won't have a dog's chance. I don't say you won't find some way to give us a bad toss, as you've done before."

"You anticipate that Bob Longworthy will be tried for the murder of Henry Coldwater, and that I shall be the solicitor for the defence? It is a position which I am unable to visualise."

"You mean you'll refuse the case?"

Inspector Combridge looked, as he asked this, as though the previous anxiety with which he had regarded the prospective prosecution had suddenly left his mind.

"I should be grateful if you would understand me to have meant precisely what I said, neither less nor more."

"Well, we're going to arrest him, so if you didn't mean that—"

"Then I must have meant something a little different."

It may have been with a deliberate intention of changing the subject of conversation that Mr. Jellipot added: "I see Flipp got bail yesterday."

"Yes. We opposed it as hard as we could. But he's got money to spend, and if he hadn't got it from the magistrate he'd have got it from a judge in chambers, more likely than not; so we had to be content with getting it fixed high. But we should have opposed it more than we did if I'd had that talk with Dawes twenty-four hours earlier."

"I should have thought, if you have him well watched, he might be of more use to you outside than in."

"Yes. We shan't overlook that."

Inspector Combridge departed with a vague feeling of buoyancy, as though he walked beneath a heaven of clearing clouds, and Mr. Jellipot relapsed into his mood of hesitation regarding the defence of Bob Longworthy, which had not been simplified by the revelations of Sneaky Dawes.

He was still in that mood of indecision—or it might be more accurate to say that he had decided definitely not to give a decisive answer—when Mrs. Renshaw was announced next morning.

"I hope," she said, coming straight to the point at once, "that you have decided to help us."

"If you mean by that, in the event of your son being charged with the murder of Henry Coldwater, will I undertake his defence, I can only reply that the position has not arisen, and may possibly never arise, and I cannot pledge myself in advance. Should he be arrested, he, or you, could approach me then, if you should still be of the same mind. But I can imagine reasons why it would be better for you to go elsewhere."

Mrs. Renshaw appeared to be both puzzled and disappointed by this reply, but yet to accept it without further urgency, or making any effort to ascertain what it might mean.

"I am very sorry," she said, "that you cannot promise more than that, but I must, of course, accept your decision. Do you, perhaps, think that I may be too apprehensive as to the attentions of the police? It would be a particularly unfortunate mistake to make, because Bob's holidays commence next Monday, and, in the ordinary course, we should have gone away together."

"I could not advise you to make any definite arrangements. Where were you proposing to go?"

"Nowhere particular. It would only be a matter of taking out a licence for the car."

"You mean that you would have been going on a motoring tour?"

"Yes. It has been a yearly custom. We have all gone together. I am fond of motoring. I have been so ever since I did a lot of driving in Prance during the war. But the car has been laid up at Lawson's Garage to save expense for the last six months. Jessica couldn't have come this time, because of the shop, but Bob needs the holiday, and I thought, if you were to tell the police that we intend—"

"I don't think it would be wise to propose that. It might be better for your son to decide to stay quietly at home on this occasion."

"Very well. I must take your advice. But it's rather hard on Bob, who only gets one holiday in the year."

Mr. Jellipot did not dispute that. But he thought that Bob Longworthy would be arrested before Monday came, and that he was doing no more than prevent abortive preparations being commenced. Actually, his forecast was not correct, for the warrant was held back by official caution while the opinion of the Attorney-General was obtained.

CHAPTER XXIV.

THE APPEARANCE OF MR. BRICE

MR. JELLIPOT heard the cheerful voice of his articled clerk on the telephone from the outer office: "There's a gentleman and lady to see you, sir. Mr. Charles Brice and Mrs. Lee."

"Very well, Richard. Show them in."

In the brief interval that elapsed before the visitors were announced, he considered the implications of Mr. Brice's unexpected appearance. He had written to Jessica Lee, suggesting that she should call upon him to discuss a letter which he had received, requesting him to supply a schedule of the goods claimed, with a statement of the circumstances under which Miss Lee contended that they had passed into her possession; to which, in view of the increasing gravity of the whole position, he had decided that he could not reply without a personal interview. He had looked forward to meeting Miss Lee with some curiosity of anticipation; for while he thought that he had made a safe guess as to the circumstances of Henry Coldwater's abrupt decease, he was still in considerable doubt as to the degree of Miss Lee's innocence, or the full extent and nature of her indiscretions; and he felt that, if his judgment should have gone wrong in other directions, it would be from this uncertainty that its error sprang.

But he had not asked for, not anticipated, a second visitor. He remembered that Inspector Combridge had told him that Mrs. Renshaw had described Mr. Charles Brice as a young man who would not be late at his work though the heavens fell. He concluded that he had not come now unless his fiancée's affairs had become of an urgent importance to his mind.

Mr. Jellipot also observed Richard Dyke's unintentional lapse from conventional phraseology: "a gentleman and lady." It was no more than reasonable deduction that it was Mr. Brice who had been forward to enquire whether he could be seen, and to furnish names.

He judged that Jessica Lee's affairs were now in firm—and he hoped discreet and honest—controlling hands.

It may have been a deliberate consequence of Jessica's shyness that Charles Brice entered before her. Mr. Jellipot saw a neat, slender man, quietly self-possessed, with small dark-brown eyes very deeply set in a thin, colourless face. Knowing what he did already about him, it was easy to recognise in face and manner the research-worker rather than the commercial or professional man.

Beyond that, he had a reserve behind the cool confidence of his address which Mr. Jellipot found difficult to penetrate or to understand. His first thought on hearing his name announced had been that he would be interesting to meet. He was a young man, presumably of good character and in a highly respectable occupation, who had wooed Jessica unsuccessfully before Henry Coldwater had appeared on the scene. But while she had been unresponsive to Charlie Brice, she had fallen so far under the influence of the older man that she had allowed him to seduce her under a promise of marriage which may never have been seriously meant, and, as a result of that imprudence, she was now obviously carrying his child.

Yet after this episode, Coldwater being dead, Charlie Brice had appeared on the scene again, with an unaltered devotion, and—perhaps less surprisingly—the girl had met him in a different mood, either because his constancy had stirred an answering passion in herself, or, more probably, because she was glad of any honourable protection that would condone the consequences of her previous folly.

But, as the interview progressed, Mr. Jellipot's feeling changed. His first object had been to form a first-hand opinion of the young client for whom he was instructed to act, and to assure himself both of the prudence of what he was doing on her behalf, and that she understood and approved. He wished also to form his own opinion of her integrity, and whether she had been, or to what extent, a party to Coldwater's criminalities. But he found that he was talking solely to Mr. Brice, and taking instructions from him.

A question directed explicitly to her would have no more effect than to cause her eyes to lift quickly to her companion's face, inviting him to reply, which he was always ready to do. And what he said was no more than Mr. Jellipot had understood previously. Neither he nor Jessica, he asserted with quiet emphasis, was concerned for the worth of the goods, or attached any sentimental value to them. But they had been given to her by a man who owed her far more than his estate would ever be asked to pay, and, if she should now appear afraid to contest her right, it might be misinterpreted in a manner he did not wish her to risk.

Mr. Jellipot saw that such an attitude might be genuine, and even if it were not so it might be politic to adopt. He took Mr. Brice's instructions without demur, but he resolved, even before the interview terminated, that he would take the unusual course of calling upon Jessica during the following morning, when he would be likely to find her alone. He saw that, even apart from any exceptional influence under which the girl might have fallen, it was improbable that she would be disposed to talk freely to him, in the presence of her present fiancé, concerning her relations with the dead man.

As the brief interview was rather stiffly terminating, Mr. Jellipot's pertinacity, overcoming timidity with more than its usual effort, forced him to say: "I understood from Mrs. Renshaw that you are getting married almost immediately?"

The girl's eyes were lifted to her lover, who replied, with a slight thawing of geniality: "Yes. We have fixed it for Thursday of next week."

"Then you will permit me to wish you every possible happiness."

Mr. Brice responded conventionally. The girl said nothing, but looked faintly, shyly, pleased.

Mr. Jellipot became suddenly aware that his judgment was formed. She had not been Coldwater's accomplice, but his victim, fascinated, flattered, deceived. He thought also that he would have her confidence if he could talk to her alone, and confirmed his resolution to see her on the following day. But of the wisdom of the hasty marriage he was less sure.

CHAPTER XXV.

Jessica States Her Own Case

IT was Thursday morning when Charlie Brice and Jessica called upon Mr. Jellipot, and he found it to be impossible to leave his office on the following day for a sufficient length of time to make the call on which he had resolved. But he was at liberty after an hour of the clearing of his desk which was the usual Saturday morning routine, and with a thought of wonder at himself for the sacrifice he was prepared to make in a matter which was of no personal and only limited professional interest, he put aside till a later hour the anticipated pleasure of spending the rest of the summer day in the peaceful atmosphere of the Jordans beech woods, and the pleasant (and scarcely less peaceful) society of Miss Prudence Manly, boarded a No. 15 bus, and invested four pence in a ticket to Edgware Road.

Inspector Combridge almost collided with him as he got off at the corner of Praed Street, and exclaimed in some natural surprise at the encounter.

"No, I don't suppose," Mr. Jellipot replied, "that you expected to meet me here, though perhaps I ought not to be equally surprised that I see you. I shouldn't have been getting off here if I hadn't been foolish enough to suppose that all the buses that start coming up Edgware Road continue along it as far as I want to go."

"Then I may conclude," the inspector said, without enthusiasm, "that we are on the way to the same address."

Mr. Jellipot was considering his own preferences rather than those of the detective when he replied in a similar tone: "Perhaps it will be better if I come at another time." And then, as they both stood in an awkward indecision, he added rather to maintain the conversation than in expectation of an affirmative reply: "I needn't ask whether you've got on the track of the Goffe Collection yet. You'd have let me know if you had."

"No. I can't say we have, and it's looking a bit doubtful how much use Sneaky's going to be. I'd almost thought that he might be just leading us up the garden, knowing that Coldwater's gone too far to contradict anything he invents about him. But it can't be quite as simple as that. The fact is—you've got a right to know this as Sir Reginald's solicitor—he gave us three addresses where he said he knew that Coldwater used to hide the stuff." (Mr. Jellipot made a silent note of the unspoken implication that the inspector had come upon other knowledge which he would be less ready to share.) "And the rotten fact is that two of them, whether he ever used them or not, are now in decent hands, and there's nothing there—nothing to excuse us raiding them in the way we've done—and the third is Miss Lee's shop, F. C. Halters & Co., that we know already."

"Which naturally isn't much satisfaction to you?"

"No. But it's odd. And it shows that Dawes wasn't making it all up out of his own head."

Mr. Jellipot observed the soundness of these conclusions. Mr. Dawes had been in retirement for the last two years, and could have had no knowledge of Coldwater's recent connexion with Jessica, or the stationery business. Had he been concocting a baseless tale, it seemed certain that he would not have given that address as one where the illicit plunder was stored. To that extent, it supported the reality of the tale he told. But its oddity lay in the same fact that Coldwater's occupation of the back room had commenced at so comparatively recent a date. How had Sneaky Dawes come to hear of the place at all? Well, there was one consolation, he would be available for further questioning, being at an address that he could not leave!

So Inspector Combridge observed; and added, as Mr. Jellipot clearly left to him the question of deciding which of them should give way: "You won't want me about when you're telling Miss Lee how she can wangle that furniture claim, and I can't ask you to go back all the way you've come, so I reckon I'd better get on with another job."

"It is very good of you," Mr. Jellipot replied; "but being the last day of the week, and that as far gone as it is, I should have thought you might feel that you've done enough."

"So I might, if I hadn't got something on my mind that I couldn't do at a better time. There's no forty-hours-make-a-week's work delusion at Scotland Yard."

"I suppose," Mr. Jellipot suggested, with apparent inconsequence, "that you haven't found that letting Flipp loose has done any good yet?"

"It's a bit early to answer that," was the vague and hurried answer, as Inspector Combridge turned to make for a halting bus on the other side of the road. "I wonder," he said to himself, "how he guessed that? But it's Jellipot's turn to have a shock this time, if I'm not wrong."

Mr. Jellipot thought: "They've followed Flipp somewhere that's put a new aspect on the case. But why doesn't he want me to know?" He hoped that it might be something that would suggest the inexpediency of arresting Bob Longworthy, but his judgment did not support the probability of that conclusion. Well, he must be content for the moment that he seemed likely to have a clear held for conversation with Jessica Lee!

He found her serving behind the counter, and the glance she gave him as they shook hands was evidence that she did not regard him as an unwelcome visitor. She called into the back room: "You won't be long, will you, Millie? I've got someone come to see me," and then explained: "Miss Rapp is just finishing lunch, and I've nowhere I can ask you into except that room."

Mr. Jellipot said he would wait, and took the solitary chair which was provided for the accommodation of customers. He did not feel that what was on his mind could be said in the shop, and he was able to observe, during the next ten minutes, that the interruption of serving customers would have been almost continual. They entered frequently—at least during Saturday afternoon—though the sums they spent were small. He approved her manner also, which addressed them all in a shyly intimate manner, as though they were personal friends, whose wants it was a pleasure to satisfy.

During a moment when the shop was clear, he expressed a hope that she was now making it pay, and received a hopeful reply. Only more stock was still needed. The shop was large, and so was the variety of goods in which such a business may deal. But she had been afraid to buy as much as she would have liked.

In a few minutes Millie appeared, and Jessica led her visitor into the back room.

"I thought," Mr. Jellipot said at once, in his characteristic manner, which may be not unfairly described as a diffident bluntness, "if I may say so with appearing to reflect upon the kindness of Mr. Brice in coming with you on Thursday, that I would prefer to see you alone."

Jessica said no more than "Yes," but there was no sound of objection in this monosyllabic reply.

"There are some matters," he went on, "concerning which it may be important that I should be correctly informed; and I can only feel entire certainty on that point, if I have them directly from you. May I conclude that, whatever confidence you may have felt at one time in Mr. Coldwater, that feeling has radically changed since you have learnt the true character of the man, and the nature of his occupations?"

He watched closely, as he asked this, for any sign of resentment, any disposition to champion the cause of the murdered man, whose mistress she had so recently been, and whose child she was destined to bear. He considered that such a reaction would have told him much not only as to her own character, but also that of the dead man, and of the relations that had existed between them. But he saw no indication of anything but assent, as to a proposition too obvious for discussion.

"I know now," she replied, "that he was just making use of me. But I thought differently then."

"And did you have cause to doubt, as he came here, and you got to know him better, that some of his business transactions might not be of a strictly legal kind?"

"No. Why should I? He didn't do anything wrong here. Not that I know of, anyway. Such a thought never entered my head."

"That is what I was hoping—and I may say expecting—to hear." Both the readiness and substance of her reply encouraged him to carry the inquisition on to more delicate ground. "I suppose you've known Mr. Brice quite a long while?"

"Yes. Well, fairly. He's been very good to me all along."

The tone was as though she spoke to assure herself rather than him, and he noticed that she answered more than his question had held.

"I should prefer to say that he is an exceptionally fortunate young man." Mr. Jellipot said this with sincerity. He thought her to be a charming girl, and one who would make an excellent wife. Mr. Coldwater was dead. It should not be hard to forget him. It was true that there was a child to come, but he would have said that there are worse things: and the way the business was going suggested that it need be no burden to Charlie Brice. It was not a view that all men would share, but chivalry was too natural to Mr. Jellipot for him, lawyer though he was, to regard meaner aspects, unless by a definite effort of the judicial habit which was never far from his waking thoughts.

They were both conscious of matters to which neither made open allusion, as she answered: "You see, he feels responsible, in a way, because it was he who advised me to buy the business, and he says I shouldn't have met Henry, but for that."

Mr. Jellipot recognised generosity in that view of the matter. It even went beyond reason, in its endeavour to comfort her self-esteem, or to take responsibility; for in recommending a girl to purchase a business it is not usual to consider the risk of her seduction by the estate-agent concerned. But his mind turned from that to the fact itself, which appeared to have an increased though indecipherable significance from that other puzzling fact that he had heard from Inspector Combridge in the last hour—that Sneaky Dawes had mentioned those premises as having been nefariously used by Henry Coldwater more than two years before.

"Do you mean," he asked, "that you told Mr. Brice that you were looking out for a business, and he heard of this?"

"Not exactly. It had belonged to someone—a cousin of his, I believe—who had to go abroad for his health, and had put it into Mr. Coldwater's hands to sell. And Charlie knew that I had six hundred pounds coming to me when I was eighteen, and he told me it would be a good way of investing the money. I didn't get it for that, because there was more stock to pay for than Mr. Coldwater had thought at first—we only found out afterwards that a lot of it wasn't very good—but Mother found three hundred and forty pounds, and the lawyers' costs."

"And then you found that the business wasn't worth what you had paid?"

"There wasn't much business here. There was more dirt. But," she added, wishing to be fair to all, absent or dead, "it may have gone down after Mr. Johnson fell ill, and left. There are enough people about, if we have what they want to buy."

Mr. Jellipot had been hesitating while this conversation continued as to whether he should return her confidences with one that might possibly be beneficial to her, and her last remark decided him that it could be safely and wisely done. He told her of Sneaky Dawes, of the theft of the Goffe Collection, of the supposition that it had passed into Henry Coldwater's hands, and finally of the curious suggestion that he had been using those premises for illicit purposes more than two years before.

"If that were so," he added, "you will recognise the possibility that he may have property hidden away in his own rooms which the police have not discovered, and which it might be greatly to your benefit to be the one to find, if you can think of where it could be.

"It would almost certainly be of such a character that it would have to be handed over to those from whom it had been stolen, perhaps several years ago, but the question of rewards would arise, and, particularly in the case of the Goffe Collection, the amount would be very large. It is a sum of sixteen thousand pounds."

Jessica's eyes opened widely at the mention of that figure, but fell with the reflection that the possibility of winning it was not worth serious consideration.

"I don't know," she said, "why people say things that are not true, but I can't help thinking that there's something wrong with that tale. It was only after I'd been here for some weeks that Henry first proposed using the room, and then it was because he said the pound a week he was to pay would help me to carry on.

"Of course, he may have had some different reasons from that—I suppose he had—but you know how he had to alter the room. And there's another thing. There's that man they arrested. Flipp. Inspector Combridge makes out that he knew everything that went on, and that's how it looked to me; but he didn't know about Henry having a room here, and he—Mr. Coldwater, I mean—was very angry when he found out."

"It is certainly a circumstance," Mr. Jellipot replied, "deserving of consideration. But it is one that is capable of a different construction. If Coldwater had used these premises at one time, with Flipp's knowledge, as a secret depository, and had given them up, he might think that he could come back without Flipp guessing that he would do so. If he were getting to think that the man knew rather too much it would be a quite probable thing for him to do without mentioning it, and he would be naturally angry when he found that he had wormed it out."

"Well," she said, with no conviction in her tone, "that may have been how it was, but if there were all the Crown Jewels hidden here, and all the money in the Bank of England, it wouldn't be any good to me, for Inspector Combridge means to be first. I should think you can hear that now."

Mr. Jellipot had not been unconscious, as this conversation had proceeded, of various noises of hammering, with an occasional louder rumble, and now, as Jessica spoke, she rose and led him to the back passage, and the entrance to the long divided room that Henry Coldwater had made his own.

Here a policeman guarded the door, and though Inspector Combridge might be hunting in other fields, his spirit operated within. The floor was being torn up from end to end. The walls were being sounded and drilled.

"I asked," she said, "when they began, who was going to pay for the mess, and they told me it should all be put right without troubling me, and I hope it will."

Mr. Jellipot decided that he had heard and seen enough to occupy his mind for the weekend. He said good afternoon, and went home.

CHAPTER XXVI.

CALLERS ON MR. JELLIPOT

MR. JELLIPOT gave much thought during the weekend to the affairs of Henry Coldwater as they had been during his life and subsequently, as well as to the circumstances of his abrupt decease. He confirmed his confidence in one conclusion which he had reached previously, he developed others, and he found himself in more than one insoluble doubt. But after he reached his office on Monday morning he soon found that the time for quiet reflection was past, and a week of action begun.

The performance opened, as he had not anticipated, with a visit from Jessica. She appeared to be more agitated than when he had talked with her on Saturday, as though she had come through a worrying weekend. She began abruptly: "Charlie made me promise to come to see you first thing. He says he can't understand why you allow the police to pull the building about in the way they do. He feels sure I shall be left to put it right in the end. He says you could get an injunction or something to make them stop now, and even if they got their own way in the end, we shouldn't feel quite so bad about it if we'd done all that we could."

Mr. Jellipot looked at the harassed girl in a pause of silence. He had thoughts to which he doubted the prudence of giving words. He asked "Have the police found anything, as far as you know?"

"No. I believe not. They went on till midday yesterday, and Charlie made me stay, so that they shouldn't try anything at the shop, if we weren't there. Then they went off, and said they'd done, and we mightn't see them again. They didn't look very pleased. We went back twice to see if their going was just a trick but they weren't there."

"Does Mrs. Renshaw also think that they ought to be stopped, at whatever cost, even if it could only be for a short time?"

"Mother didn't say much, one way or other. She didn't seem to care. She's so worried about Bob. That's another thing! The police never let him out of their sight. Even at the Sunday School yesterday he says there were two men watching, one at each entrance, as though they thought he might be trying to slip away. You'd think even a policeman would have more sense."

"More sense than to think he would commit a murder, or to run away?"

"Both, of course. I meant that he wouldn't kill anyone. You'd think any fool could see that."

"Murders are sometimes committed by the most unlikely people. I suppose you realise that, if he did it, it was out of a mistaken sense of loyalty to yourself?"

"But I tell you he *didn't*. He never would. He's not got the—I mean his courage isn't that kind. And he'd feel sure it was wrong! You don't know what Bob's conscience is." The girl's face changed suddenly. Her eyes were half frightened, half hostile, as she exclaimed: "You don't really think it was he?"

"No. I will go so far as to say that I am sure it was not."

"And yet Mother said when she asked you to defend him, if he were arrested, you wouldn't say yes or no?"

"I declined to say anything in advance. You mustn't take that too seriously. I don't think you need apprehend that Bob will come to any great harm. And you can tell Mr. Brice that I will ascertain whether the police intend any further excavating, and, if they do, I will consider what course of action would be wisest in your own interest. It would be foolish to make a fuss if they've left for good."

With these words, Mr. Jellipot rose and showed the girl politely to the door, feeling indisposed to continue a conversation where he might easily say something which would be occasion for later regret.

As soon as she had gone, he rang up Inspector Combridge, and learned, without mentioning her visit, that the search, in spite of its drastic nature, had been absolutely vain. For the moment, there was to be no further investigation at the shop, attention being concentrated upon Coldwater House, which was the most obvious place to choose for the hiding away of stolen goods, being a large building entirely under Coldwater's control, and with cellars that were little used.

But he also asked about Bob Longworthy, and being told that the Attorney-General's opinion, though not very confidently given, had been that a prosecution should be commenced, in consequence of which Detective-Inspector Spencer had already left to execute the warrant, he had no occasion for surprise when, about two hours later, Mrs. Renshaw called upon him.

"I expect you know," she said, "that they've arrested Bob."

"Yes. I heard this morning."

"It was a foolish thing to do."

"In a sense, yes."

Mrs. Renshaw looked as though she were disposed to challenge the obscure qualifications of this reply, relapsed to silence, opened her bag, and drew out a bundle of bearer bonds, which she laid on Mr. Jellipot's desk. "I suppose," she asked, "it wouldn't take long to get me the money for these?"

Mr. Jellipot examined them. They were of a value of about £3,000, presumably representing the capital from which Mrs. Renshaw's limited income came.

"In the ordinary course, I could get you the cash for these by next settling day. That will be Friday week."

"Wouldn't it be possible before then?"

"Yes. Perhaps at a slight extra expense. At an emergency the money could be available almost at once."

"Perhaps by Friday next?"

"Yes. Easily. Do you mean that you want me to realise these on your behalf?"

"Yes. I should like it done as quickly and quietly as possible. I suppose no one except yourself need know that they are being sold for me?"

"My clerk, Newman, will know. It need not go beyond him, and you can be sure that he does not talk."

"I don't see why that need matter."

"It is difficult to see why it should. Do you wish me to understand that you are realising these securities so that you may provide funds for your son's defence?"

"Money is needed at such times, is it not?"

"Yes. It commonly is. You will remember that I have not undertaken it?"

"I suppose there won't be much happening before Friday—before I see you again?"

"No. He will be brought before a magistrate within the next twenty-four hours, and the police will be certain to ask for a remand—probably after no more than evidence of arrest has been given."

"You will appear for him then?"

"Yes. But I promise nothing beyond that."

"That is all I ask."

Mrs. Renshaw rose as though her business were done. "Wait a moment," he said. "I can't have you going off without a receipt for the bonds.

"I don't think that matters."

"Oh, but I can assure you that it does." Mr. Jellipot smiled as he added: "You might think you have given me six thousand instead of three."

He summoned Newman, to whom he said: "Make out a receipt for these bonds. Don't copy it, and don't put Mrs. Renshaw's name on it till you bring it back for me to sign. Then take the bonds over to the bank, and say I shall want the cash for them to be here first thing on Friday morning. They won't ask whose bonds they are, coming from us, and if they do you won't say."

Newman went out to draw the receipt, and Mr. Jellipot occupied the interval of waiting with the remark: "I understood that Brice and Miss Lee had arranged to get married on Thursday. Will this make any difference to their plans?"

Mrs. Renshaw looked to be troubled by the suggestion. "Oh," she said, "I hope not! And, besides, why should it? Especially as Jessica and Bob are not really related at all."

"No. But she doesn't appear to look at things in that way. I should say that she has a strong affection for both of you—that she regards you almost as an actual mother."

"I promised her father I'd do my best. It hasn't turned out very well."

Mr. Jellipot observed that Mrs. Renshaw maintained her self-control with difficulty as she said this. He did not want her to break down in his office, nor, he was sure, did she. He restrained himself even from the obvious assurance her exclamation called for, dropping a subject on which he had meant to urge an opposite opinion from hers. He talked on indifferent topics till the receipt came, and the lady left.

CHAPTER XXVII.

MR. FLIPP AS A GOOD PARENT

THE appearance of Robert Longworthy in the magistrate's court was timed by the reporters (who, in the absence of copy, must make copy of that absence) at precisely four minutes. Detective-Inspector Spencer gave evidence of arrest. Mr. Jellipot, being asked, said that he could not object to a remand, and the adjourned hearing was fixed for the same day of the following week.

Mr. Jellipot, though he had spoken a word of encouragement to a visibly trembling, but weakly indignant prisoner, had appeared otherwise so unconcerned at anything that was happening around him, and indifferent to the date of the adjourned hearing, that Inspector Combridge, meeting him in the outer corridor, and having had a separate cause for disappointment since they had parted on Saturday afternoon in the Edgware Road, was moved to remark: "I know it's your way to go on as though the prosecution wasn't interesting you, till you drop the bomb that sends us all through the roof, but if you *know* we're wrong, I don't see why you shouldn't say it straight out. You know we don't want to—"

Mr. Jellipot, who had his own reasons for wishing to avoid an immediate discussion upon the question of who had committed the crime, interrupted with a mild but yet unusual asperity: "I fail to see why you should anticipate that I shall be willing to discuss the matter. It might be different if you had thought it worthwhile to be franker with me."

But Inspector Combridge held his ground, though he did not deny the charge. "You mean I might have said a bit more on Saturday? Well, you've got me there; but the fact was I didn't know how important it was likely to be, and in the end it turned out to be nothing at all. But I don't mind telling you what it was. I never knew a case," he concluded with an excusable irritation, "where we've had so many good-looking pointers that end up at an empty hole."

Mr. Jellipot, whose previous inclination had been to pass on with as few words as possible, now showed a more leisurely disposition. He said: "Yes. It has looked that way at times; but it isn't always easy to see what's useful and what isn't, till you've played out the whole hand."

"Well, it was about Flipp. It looked to me that you had been right when you said that we should get more on him by letting him run loose than while he was bolted in. We hadn't overlooked that. We kept a pretty close watch on him from the moment he walked out, but he gave two of our best men the slip on Friday afternoon, and it was just a bit of luck we didn't deserve that another one, who'd seen him while he was in custody, picked him up, and saw him make a call at a house where he stayed more than half an hour.

"The care he'd taken to shake our men off made it look more important than if he'd gone openly, and when we'd looked up who lived at the place, and found that it was Mr. Charles Brice, I thought something juicy might be coming our way."

"Yes," Mr. Jellipot said frankly, "I should have thought the same."

"So did I. It made it look as though—which I've always had in mind as being about as likely as not—instead of Coldwater having taken Brice's innocent sweetheart away, and sold a rotten business to her and her simple family, they may have all been in the gang, and just staged it in that way to put the blinkers on us, if we should get smelling round—I mean before Coldwater got that steel under his ribs. It sounds silly now I've got at the facts, but that's how it looked then."

"Yes," Mr. Jellipot agreed again, feeling no disposition to criticise this conclusion. Knowing, as he did, that the business of F. C. Halters & Co. had been introduced to Jessica by Charlie Brice, the fact that Flipp was anxious to visit him while on bail might have had an even more definitely sinister aspect to his mind than that in which Inspector Combridge admitted that it had appeared to him. But he said nothing of this, waiting with an open mind for the explanation to come.

"Of course," the inspector went on, "suspicion's no good to us, unless we can give it a definite shape, and we're still badly wanting a little more direct evidence against Theo Flipp, so I thought my best way would be to go to Brice and ask him straight out what business Flipp had with him, and then go at once to Flipp, and ask him the same question. Unless they both refused to talk, or told the same tale, I thought it might give a start on one of those roads that end up a long way from where they begin.

"Well, I dropped on Mr. Brice rather sharp, and shouldn't have been surprised if he'd been a bit confused, but he seemed not to care one way or other, and as to why Mr. Flipp had called on him, he said he couldn't see any reason why he should mind him saying.

"He said he met Flipp casually more than once when he's been at the shop, and the man had told him that his eldest boy, who is just at school-leaving age, is mad on chemistry, and asked him if he could use his influence to get him a job at Hart & Peasley's. He says he hadn't promised anything, as he didn't take to Flipp particularly; he had just put him off without giving a final yes or no, but when he came to him on Friday night, he definitely declined. He says that Flipp went on begging for some time, but he told him that he didn't know the boy, and he must apply, if at all, on his own merits, without reference to him.

"It sounded genuine enough, but I wasn't taking anything without proof. I went straight to Flipp's house, and as he wasn't in, I tackled the wife, and had just the same tale from her. So that's that. And if I'd had the sense to go home at the proper time I should have been doing a useful afternoon's work in the garden instead of wasting it as I did."

Mr. Jellipot did not deny that; but it was with an air of fully recovered serenity that he remarked: "Perhaps, as you have been kind enough to explain what has, I own, been an object of some mental speculations—which I may add were wildly wrong—during the weekend, I ought to tell you that I am not at all disposed to think that, apart from the fact that he is a quite innocent boy, you have made any mistake in arresting Longworthy on the present charge." And then observing that this cryptic commendation had reduced the inspector to a momentary dumbness, such as might have an explosive sequel in the next minute, he hastened to add: "But I mustn't keep you longer now. I expect we shall be meeting again tomorrow? Yes, Sir Reginald has asked me to be present. It's like old times for us all to be on the same trail. Not," he concluded modestly, "that Sir Reginald can be looking for any help on such a matter from me, unless there should be any point of law which I may be useful in looking up."

CHAPTER XXVIII.

The Opinions of Sir Reginald Crowe

SIR REGINALD received his visitors with the friendliness that past and present acquaintance required, and with the courtesy due to one of the Bank's principal solicitors, and to a Chief Inspector of the C.I.D.; but it was evident that he was not one who took disappointment patiently.

"We're hard at work now," Inspector Combridge added, when he had explained the negative result of the best information that Sneaky Dawes appeared able to give, "on Coldwater House, and in the next twenty-four hours we shall be able to tell you definitely whether there's anything hidden there."

"Which, of course," Sir Reginald retorted, "there won't be. You don't think that with all the care Coldwater took over smaller things, and that made mugs of you—I don't mean to be rude, but you know that's the right word—as long as he lived, that he was fool enough to have those stamps on his own premises, where they would mean seven years for him any time they were turned up? You'll have to get on to something better than that before I start writing cheques for you or anyone else in this connection."

"We're not asking for any cheques," Inspector Combridge replied, "and you know we can't take them unless we get the Assistant Commissioner's consent. We're just doing our job the best we can for its own sake, and if we can recover the Goffe Collection we're glad to do it, whether we get any thanks or not."

"It sounds very noble," the banker replied, with a smile that took much of the sting from the spoken word, "but you know what my opinion is. There'd be more sense in giving you ten percent of all the stolen property you get back; and if the first object is to discourage crime it would be good policy to make it more than that, up to half the swag.

"You can lay Coldwater House flat, and crumble the mortar between the bricks, but you'll find nothing there to interest me. And why you're persecuting that poor youngster who had the pluck to kill a scoundrel who was too much for you—"

It was a thought so monstrous that words failed even the habitual fluency of the chairman of the London & Northern Bank.

"We're not persecuting anyone," Inspector Combridge replied, with a stubborn patience which refused either to take offence, or to admit the justice of the banker's half-jesting strictures. "If there's any persecuting, it's not us, it's the law, and we don't make the law, and we don't administer it either. But if we find one murdering another, we take charge of him, and get the facts, and the law does what it thinks just, which we mayn't like any better than you."

"Nonsense, Combridge! You know perfectly well that you didn't find anyone murdering Coldwater. I don't say what you should have done if you had. I should have given him all the loose cash I had on me to help him to get away. But you can't leave well alone. I'd bet anything that you've actually been losing sleep worrying how you could patch up a case against that boy that would land him where he is now, and make more misery in a world that was bad enough without that, with the Nazis beheading people who try to get their own money out of Germany, and this new trouble with the Chilean exchange!"

Inspector Combridge was wise enough not to continue the argument further. He hit back with some dexterity, asking bluntly: "Well, if you think we're wasting time on Coldwater House, perhaps you'll tell me what you'd do if you were in our place?"

He thought it to be a position in which criticism was much easier than constructive advice, but Sir Reginald had no difficulty in his reply.

"Cultivate the girl, Combridge! Pump the girl! You know how much Coldwater was with her, and on what terms they were. He's almost certain to have let out something in all those weeks. Anyone would. Something that would put you on the right track, though she mightn't see where it leads. You ought to have let everything else go so that you could be really pally with her. And instead of that you try to hang the young man who knifed the scoundrel who got her into the mess! And he a boy who'd been brought up with her, and she might have married more likely than not, and the whole thing ended up in a happy way."

"She hadn't any intention of marrying him," Inspector Combridge replied, meeting the first point which he could definitely refute. "She's engaged herself to another man."

"Which only shows that women don't know their own minds. What do you say, Jellipot? Haven't I talked more sense than a policeman often has the good fortune to hear?"

Mr. Jellipot, who had been listening to a conversation which he was more interested to hear than to interrupt, replied cautiously: "The policy which you urge, Sir Reginald, is not one on which I feel any competence to give an opinion, beyond saying that though it may be sound as a generalisation, I doubt its applicability to the present case.

"I have reached a decided conclusion that Coldwater was extremely cautious and far-seeing, and in the course of posing successfully—as I am sure he did—to Miss Lee as a conventional business man, I should think it extremely improbable that he made even the remotest allusion to the place where the Goffe Collection is doubtless most securely hidden.

"But I must admit that the idea that the two young people should marry had not occurred to me previously, and it has a good deal in its favour.

"I suppose it is hardly worth saying that the boy had neither the courage nor the disposition to have murdered Coldwater, yet he showed considerable courage of his own sort in going to tackle him in the way he did; and though it is true that Miss Jessica is, for the moment, engaged to another man, that is no evidence that Bob may not be in love with her."

Mr. Jellipot's two auditors spoke at once.

"You seem to be very sure that we've got the wrong man in the dock."

"I judge, Jellipot, that the girl's engagement is one of which you do not warmly approve?"

Mr. Jellipot answered them with his usual precision.

"I have told you already, Inspector, that I don't think you know where you're going, but it doesn't follow that you're not on the right road. But as to Miss Lee's engagement, there's nothing whatever to be said against the young man, whose constancy and persistence may be said to deserve the reward that they are expected to get, but I have formed the opinion that she is only marrying him because she doesn't want the child to be born without having a proper name, and perhaps because she doesn't think she would easily marry elsewhere after she'd told the truth, which she would be certain to do.

"But she would make an excellent wife for Robert Longworthy, being almost twenty years older already than he is ever likely to be."

"I hope," Sir Reginald said, "that you don't mean by that that you think the law—"

"No. I think he is more likely to die of old age. But I should like to say that I am very glad to have had the benefit of this stimulating conversation. It has given me an idea which, I must confess, had not entered my mind previously. And so far as the Goffe Collection is concerned, Sir Reginald, I don't think I would give up hope that it may be recovered."

"I am not giving up hope at all. And if I had done, I should feel differently after hearing you say that. You've got brains, and in your heart you don't care for the law any more than I do. It's no use looking so shocked, Jellipot. It's the truth, though you mayn't have guessed it before. And you mustn't take anything I've said, Combridge, in the wrong way. I admire the Metropolitan Police almost as much as though I were an American visitor. But I bought the Goffe Collection as a present for my wife on our first wedding anniversary—the only stamps I take any interest in myself are those that ornament bills of exchange—and I've been down late for breakfast because I've been ashamed to look her in the face every morning from then till now."

With these words, Sir Reginald Crowe, having relieved his feelings sufficiently, and having a far greater confidence in the ability of Inspector Combridge than his picturesque fluency had implied, rose briskly, to indicate the conclusion of the conference.

Mr. Jellipot excused himself, as he left, from further conversation with the inspector, on the genuine ground that he had other most urgent business upon his mind. For the remainder of the afternoon he was obliged to put the Coldwater case aside, and it was only after he had reached home, and the evening was far advanced, that he laid down his after-dinner cigar to pick up his fireside telephone and ask to be put through to Paddington 6669.

CHAPTER XXIX.

The Interference of Mr. Jellipot

"PADDINGTON 6669. Miss Williams speaking."

"Is Mrs. Renshaw in?"

"No. I believe not. Can I take any message for her?"

"Is Mrs. Lee in?"

"Yes. I think so."

"Please put me through to her." Next moment Mr. Jellipot heard Jessica's voice. He asked: "Are you alone?"

"Yes. Quite. I am expecting Mr. Brice any minute, but I'm alone now."

"Then will you forgive me if I ask a question which you may say is no business of mine? Have you decided to, or have you seriously considered, putting off the ceremony which I understood that you were arranging for tomorrow, in view of—"

The girl's voice that interrupted him sounded uncertain and troubled. "No. Do you think I ought? You don't mean that you think Bob will be convicted, do you? It doesn't seem possible to believe that. I offered to release Charlie, if he thought that with—everything—he'd rather not go on with it, but he wouldn't hear of that. He says I shall need him to look after me all the more."

There was a note of satisfaction, even of pride, in the girl's voice as she said this, which Mr. Jellipot recognised to be natural enough. But he judged also that the delay, in itself, would be a cause less for regret than relief, and it encouraged him to urge that which, as he had admitted, was no apparent business of his, and which, beyond that, he would have regarded as unreasonable had the case been presented to him for his opinion in an abstract form.

"I can understand Mr. Brice looking at it in that way," he replied, "and so far as Bob is concerned, I don't think you need have any fear that he will not be ultimately exonerated; but all the same, I would most urgently advise you, Mrs. Lee"—he was careful to use the married style of address, not knowing, with such a telephone, who might be listening-in—"in your ultimate interest, and for reasons which I cannot discuss on the telephone, to postpone the marriage until your—until Robert Longworthy is released."

"May I say that I am acting on your advice, if I do that?"

"No. Please do not. It would be most unwise, and, I think, make your position more difficult. Mr. Brice would be certain to resent what he would regard as an unwarranted interference on my part. But I am sure that, if you will stand firm now, you will see that you have done wisely when you look back upon these events at a later day."

"Ye-es. I expect you are right. I don't know how, but I suppose—" The hesitant voice broke off, and the connection was cut. Mr. Jellipot guessed correctly that Mr. Brice had entered the room.

He was left uncertain of whether his counsel had prevailed. If it had not, he could do no more. It was Wednesday evening now. The next morning they were to be married at the Registry Office. He could not think that it would be an ideal union. But he owned to himself that that had not been the sole, perhaps not the primary, consideration on which he had acted. If the marriage should take place in spite of the urgent advice he had given, he would have to reconsider the whole position, for it was reasonably certain that the development on which he was counting would not occur.

But Mr. Jellipot, in spite of this open doubt, could lean back and enjoy the remainder of his interrupted cigar. For the time, he had nothing more to do, and very little of which to think, while Jessica, whom he had sent into the firing-line of a battle the purpose of which she did not understand, had a less pleasant time.

Charlie Brice had come to see her on the last evening before their marriage in good temper with himself and with a world which went well for him. He was not demonstrative, whether of disposition or because he had wit to see that she had, as yet, no warmer feeling for him than a natural gratitude for loyalty under circumstances which would have caused many suitors to withdraw. Such a feeling must be fanned gently if it is to be roused to a brighter flame.

Still, on the last evening, he embraced and kissed her with some warmth, to which she was nervous in her response. She knew herself well enough to be aware that, unless she should be instant to speak what was in her mind, it would not be said. She knew her courage would not endure.

"Charlie," she said hurriedly, "I know you'll be dreadfully angry, but I've been thinking things over, and I'm sure it will be best to put it off. Anyway, for a short time, till we see what's going to happen."

The expression that crossed his face as he heard this certainly justified her prediction, though it might be said that it had cause. But he controlled himself to reply: "Angry with you, darling? Of course not! I'm not going to hear a word of such nonsense. If I don't see any reason to put it off—" He ended the unfinished sentence with a kiss which she took passively.

"But you did see *some* reason," she replied, striving to find logical support for that which was being decided illogically. "You must have done, or you wouldn't have said that we had better have it quietly, without going away."

That was a fact. The first plan was that the marriage should be should take place quietly at the Registry Office, and should be followed by a brief seven-day holiday at Bexhill. But last week, when it had become evident that the police were concentrating their attention upon Bob, and she had first asked him (then anticipating nothing but a protest of denial) whether he would not wish to postpone the marriage, he had given the expected assurance, but coupled it, rather surprisingly to her, with a suggestion that, under the circumstances, they should not go away. She could come at once to his present apartment, which had been their plan on returning, until the rooms at the back of the shop could be refitted and furnished to make a temporary, if not permanent home.

Neither she nor Mrs. Renshaw, with whom she had talked it over, had seen reason in this. If family troubles could be ignored sufficiently for the marriage to take place, it did not seem to make much difference whether they were ignored at Bexhill or in the neighbourhood of the Edgware Road. But Mrs. Renshaw, who had been evidently anxious that the ceremony should not be postponed, had counselled acquiescence. "If he doesn't seem anxious to get away," she had said.

"He says we shall enjoy hurrying the alterations on at the shop. He wants me to take out the electric fire in the living-room for one thing—he says he hates them—and open up the chimney for a coal-fire again."

"I thought he had electric fires in his own rooms."

"He says that's how he's got to hate them the way he does. Besides that, they are so dear."

"Well, they are dear. On the other hand, they save trouble. But I should let him have it the way he wants."

"Oh, yes, I didn't mind that. I said we'd give an order for that last week, but I thought we'd better get the police out of the way first, if they looked like going. They hadn't begun pulling up floors then."

"Well, anyway, if he seems not to want you to go away—he may have work at the laboratories that's not easy to leave."

So it had been agreed. But now, when he heard it brought up against himself, though it brought a look of vexation to his face, he put it easily aside.

"I only proposed that because I thought you might prefer not to be away, and not know what might be going on here. You mustn't turn that against me, because I tried to think what you would like."

"I'm not turning anything against you. I'm only sorry you're going to marry into a family that's got itself into such a mess. But I don't want you to do that until things are a bit straighter than they are now."

"And I say you need someone to look after you all the more. And if I'm anxious for it to go on, and you say you're only thinking of me—"

So they argued for the next hour. More than once she was on the threshold of giving way. In her heart she knew that she would have yielded had she desired the marriage with normal passion, with the love which she should have felt. She knew also that she would not have had sufficient courage or obstinacy to resist his pleading, and deny the promise already made, had not the influence of Mr. Jellipot's advice been upon her, the urgent tone of his voice being like a mental pressure that would not lift.

Even so, Charlie would have been likely to have his way, had not his hardly restrained anger led him to threaten her that, if she would not marry at this time, she might find that another would never come. It was an argument which might have been potent had her love for the man who spoke it been of a stronger and more natural growth, even without the thought that, in five months' time, she would be destined to bear an otherwise nameless child, but feeling mentally and physically wearied as she did, it gave her the excuse for anger which the weakness of her arguments required. Words were said of a sharpness that she knew to be unjust, but would not recall.

When, seeing his error, he showed an apparent willingness to compromise, and suggested that, if tomorrow *must* be abandoned, they might discuss it again in a day or two, when there might be sufficient change in circumstance or herself to allow of a different conclusion, she said that she would rather leave the subject entirely. Anyhow, for tonight. She was tired. She might change her mind altogether. It was no use saying any more now.

He went at that, in a mood of anger he no longer made effort to check. He left her half wretched and half relieved.

When Mrs. Renshaw came in, Jessica told her what had occurred, to the older woman's evident distress. "I can't think," she said, "why Mr. Jellipot should have interfered. If you and Charlie were agreed, I don't see why it should matter to him."

Jessica was unable to explain that. She felt a miserable doubt as to whether she had not added another to the disastrous blunders with which her life was opening. Why was she so easily influenced by others? Even now, when she had stood firm against masculine persuasion, the impulse had come from another mind. At that moment, had Charlie Brice been there, she might have taken back all she had said, and she would certainly have found him willing to do the same. But he had gone, and his mind was busy with other plans.

CHAPTER XXX.

MR. FLIPP IS PREPARED FOR FLIGHT

MR. BRICE'S rooms were in Kensington. They were so spacious and comfortable, he having some private income, apart from the salary which he received for his laboratory labours, that Jessica had had a natural wonder when he had first spoken of giving them up, and living, after their marriage, behind the shop. She had recognised that the time might be too short for securing and furnishing a house, and such an expenditure might be, for all she knew, beyond his immediate resources. But still—was he, she had wondered miserably, ashamed to introduce to the landlady and her staff a wife who was so evidently carrying a child on her wedding day? Perhaps it was natural enough! Although the tale of sudden widowhood which they had agreed to tell—

But she had done him injustice. He had had a different, though it might be wrong to describe it as a more worthy, motive.

It was his habit, after leaving Amptill Terrace, to go home across the park, if it were not closed, finding an evening walk to be pleasant and beneficial. He might even make the circuit through Notting Hill. He walked now, but blindly, needing time for thought, and for a decision that must be made.

He went down Oxford Street, and had reached the corner of Tottenham Court Road when his resolution was formed. It was a risk that he did not like. But it was for a great gain. And he was not sure that inaction might not lead to a danger even greater, and against which his wits would be of no avail.

He took a postcard from his wallet. It was addressed in typescript to Theophilus Flipp. There was nothing strange in his having that. It had been pressed upon him, already stamped, by the father of the embryo scientist, so that he could notify a change of mind, if he should decide that he could do anything for a brilliant boy! It could be proved, if necessary, that the address had been typed by Mr.

Flipp on his own machine. But it was not reasonably likely that it would be necessary to prove anything about it. Why should it? The matter had been explained—a most natural explanation—to Inspector Combridge already. And, anyway, the card was passing out of his possession now. He crossed the road, and dropped it into the box on the farther side.

After that action, there could be nothing to connect it with him. It would not even have the Kensington postmark, though there had been no intention in that. He had been walking at random, while he considered the provoking and dangerous position—but with some splendid possibilities!—into which he had been forced by Henry Coldwater's death.

As to the card being blank, it was easy to put it into the post, ready stamped as it was, overlooking the fact that he had not yet written upon it. No one could deny that. But the thought was mere folly. How—under what circumstances—should anyone be interested in the card at all? How should they connect it with him? In any case, explanation was something he could not be forced to give. There is nothing criminal in posting a stamped card, even though you may have forgotten to write upon it. He walked down Charing Cross Road still in some doubt of the decision he had taken. Suppose he had told her that he could make her a rich woman? There cannot be many girls who would not be influenced by that. But he was not sure about Jessica.

And if the argument should have failed, he would have gone near to giving himself dangerously away. Besides that, he was avoiding the nuisance of the marriage. Dangerous, too, for it might have become necessary to make away with her in the end, and there would have been the miscarriage to arrange almost at once. It was only the ultra caution that his uncle, Henry Coldwater, had taught that had made him hesitate at all. And he knew it was that elaborate caution which was his safety now. Even his relationship was unguessed by the prying officers of the C.I.D., who would not leave an investigation, even when it had become apparent that they were up against a mystery that they could not solve. Well, it was their job! He did not blame them for that. He had his job, too. And it was one in which he could not afford to fail. He had reached Leicester Square Station now, and went home by the Piccadilly Tube.

As the postcard had only been posted in time for the midnight collection, it did not reach Mr. Flipp until the second delivery, which, in his suburban district, took place at about ten-thirty. He observed the blankness of its surface without apparent surprise, though he subsequently subjected it to a close examination, even holding it up to the light to assure himself that its simplicity was absolute.

Having assured himself of that, he destroyed the card, and went to the kitchen, where Mrs. Flipp was superintending the preparation of the midday meal.

"Eva," he said, "I want to speak to you for a few minutes."

His wife, whose confidence in a husband who had always been good to her had not been shaken by the events of the last month, wiped her hands on her apron, and followed him into the front room.

"I've just had," he began at once, "an important letter. It offers me that chance of making money abroad that I told you about some time ago, but I shall lose it if I stay here till I've got rid of this difficulty with the police. Of course, I don't want to do that."

"No dear, of course not," she echoed, loyal though apprehensive. She already understood that, with Henry Coldwater's death, their comfortable income had ceased. It rendered it doubly important that this vaguely profitable position "abroad" should not be lost. In face of this "trouble with the police," temporary as he had assured her that it would be, it was difficult to see how that risk could be averted, but she had confidence in him, that he would be equal to find a way.

"I shall be going out some time this afternoon," he went on, "and if I can arrange matters the way I expect, I shall go at once; but it will be best that I should inform the police in my own way. I'm not saying I shan't be back. I don't know. And if I don't tell you more now, it's only because everything's uncertain; and I don't want you to be bothered by the police to tell them anything, if they come here before they've heard definitely from me. So if they should call, you'll just say that I'm not in, and leave it at that.

"In any case, you'll hear from me before long, and meanwhile there's fifty pounds here, and Aunt Ruth has two hundred that she'll let you have any time. But you'd better get it from her as you need it, if I'm not back, not all at once. But long before you'll have used that I shall be here again, or you'll be coming over to me."

Vaguely excited at the thought that she was to be put in sole control of so large a sum of money (for her husband had always dealt with the household expenditure, and had ruled it with an exact though not always ungenerous hand)—vaguely relieved that they would escape the publicity of the trial, which she had secretly dreaded, though without questioning the verdict that would result—vaguely troubled at the thought of the first separation of their married life, temporary though she supposed it to be—Eva Flipp showed the good results that come from marital discipline firmly though kindly exercised over a course of years, as she answered meekly: "Yes, Theo, I understand." And then asked: "What shall I say to Mr. Benson, if he looks in?"

Mr. Benson, a kind-hearted but nervous neighbour, was one of the two sureties, each for £500, whom, in addition to Mr. Flipp's own recognisances for £250, an implacable magistrate had required as the price of the temporary freedom which he was putting to so dubious a use. After being persuaded, largely by the sight of Mrs. Flipp's distress, to become surety for one of the substantial amounts demanded, Mr. Benson had developed a curiosity as to Mr. Flipp's movements which required to assure itself at least twice a day that he was still available to the requirements of the police.

"You needn't worry about him," he replied easily, "I'm going in to see him myself." In fact, Mr. Flipp's codes of honour and honesty, though they were elastic in many directions, did not permit him to jump his bail without indemnifying those who had provided it for him, which, as a result of his services to Henry Coldwater for the past ten years, and some profitable sidelines resulting therefrom, he was well able to do. But it was a matter that must be handled with discretion, for he did not propose to risk his flight being communicated to the police before they would have discovered it by their own methods.

He called upon Mr. Benson during the afternoon. He said: "Benson, I can see you're a bit nervous about that bond. I don't blame you for that. I know how I should feel. But I can't bear you to be worried because of what you've undertaken for me.

"I've brought you five hundred pounds in bank notes that you can hand back to me when the risk's over; and meanwhile you'll know that you've not got any loss to fear."

Mr. Benson said, rather weakly, that there was no need for that. He hadn't really been anxious; it was only that it was a sum that it would have been extremely inconvenient to find. And his wife had been worrying. Mr. Flipp knew what women were!

"Well, don't tell her I've brought you the cash," Mr. Flipp answered rather sharply, "because I believe it might get me into trouble, might even mean that the bail wouldn't be renewed next Wednesday, and there'd be no joke for me in that. It's better to say nothing to anyone about a little matter like this."

Mr. Benson promised to keep a still tongue, and Mr. Flipp went back to say good-bye to a tearful Eva, and to put in practice the plans which were already matured for such an emergency in his fertile mind.

CHAPTER XXXI.

A MEETING IN CROMWELL ROAD

ON the two previous days, Mr. Flipp had been amusing himself, and exasperating those subordinate but ambitious members of the Metropolitan detective force who had been detailed to observe his movements, by giving them the slip and then turning up again with a promptitude that showed him to have acted without intention of avoiding their vigilance for any serious purpose.

It was maddening for two young detectives, who had to return to headquarters with the humiliating report that he had eluded their combined attention by an adroit use of the lifts in one of the major London stores, to learn that he had arrived home so soon after this alert performance that he must have returned there by the speediest route, as one whose morning exercises had been satisfactorily performed.

Exasperated they might be, and a policy of deliberately annoying the police is not one which can be recommended to accused persons without important qualifications, but what remedy could they have? Bail is bail. They had no legal duty to follow him. He had no legal obligation to allow them to keep him in view. If he chose to treat their curiosity as a parlour game, there was no power in England to penalise him for so doing.

Actually, he had, as he considered, a sufficient motive for what he did. He had no intention of standing a trial which might result in his being put away for a period which he estimated at from two to five years, according to the degree of success which the prosecution would have in connecting him with the more serious of Henry Coldwater's criminal occupations. His star turns of evasion were still untried. He wished, when he did go, that the police, having been tricked before in an idle way, would not be hasty to take alarm.

But it was not till he received the morning's postcard that he had expected to have to arrange so speedy a disappearance, or to

159

have so much need of an untraced and unsuspected start. He had thought that it would be a matter of waiting until he had received a very substantial sum of money from Charlie Brice—probably not until after the next remand—and then making a straightforward bolt. But it seemed that the course of events was to be less easy than that.

He had confidence in himself, but he remembered the amazing luck—he could interpret it in no other way—by which the police had observed his call upon Mr. Brice during the previous week, and he determined that, on this occasion, he would make sure.

On the morning after the murder of Henry Coldwater, he had secured possession of an unconsidered key of certain vacant premises which were on the estate-agency books, but which were never advertised and consequently never let. He also removed all reference to those premises from the business files, where Mr. Coldwater had been careful to have them innocently preserved. The potential usefulness of these premises, as they had been estimated in Mr. Coldwater's precautionary dispositions, was that they ran through from one street to another, at a point where there was no near entry or alleyway which could be used as an alternative route by an observant officer of the law. As a means of shaking off unwelcome pursuit, such as aimed at observation rather than arrest, they were therefore, for the first time that they would be used, of an almost absolute utility. It was evidence of the extreme caution that Mr. Flipp had learnt from his deceased employer that he did not make his way to these premises until he had used all his previous tricks, and was confident that he was already clear of observation. Finally, having passed through the vacant premises, he hailed a passing taxi, and was driven to an address he gave, which was that of an unoccupied furnished flat in the Cromwell Road. He found that Mr. Brice was already there.

"I hope," he said, having less confidence in the caution of others than in his own, "that you have not been followed."

Mr. Brice said that he was quite sure about that. He had had a day of leisure, having already arranged to be absent from his laboratories for the marriage which had not taken place. He had occupied it in prolonged wanderings about London, ranging widely, and putting the question of surveillance to many tests. On two occasions, he had entered a Tube train at quiet stations, and then jumped up, as though becoming aware that he had chosen the wrong route, and left it just as the doors were closing. In neither case would there have been time for anyone who watched him to duplicate the performance, and he had been left, on both occasions, on an empty platform.

Mr. Flipp professed himself satisfied. He said: "Well, what's run us off the rails? Has the girl jibbed?"

"Yes. I don't know what got at her yesterday. She's behaving like a sick mule."

"You don't think that a day or two—"

"No. I don't. I don't think she means to go through with it at all. Anyway, I thought we'd better give up the idea, and go ahead our own way."

Mr. Flipp could not question the wisdom of that. Time, with that prosecution looming ahead, was what he, in particular, could not afford to lose. And there was always the danger that the police would blunder upon the secret which, even to these two, was no more than a deduction of probabilities. He said: "I reckon we'd better be there about eleven. We don't want to risk anyone being still there, nor being late enough for the streets to be getting empty.

"That gives us about an hour to get our plans settled before we start."

"I don't see how we can plan anything until we see what we find, and how difficult it will be to move. If there's not more than we can carry without raising suspicion—"

"There'll be more than that. The Goffe Collection alone—"

"If it's there."

"If it's there, of course. But so it will be, if anything is. And the Collinson tiara, more likely than not."

"Then we must risk a taxi to get them here, or else wait till Jessica arrives, and fix it with her."

"Would you risk that?"

"I don't know that I would, after what I had from her tonight. We shall have to leave some of it, more likely than not."

"I don't agree about that. My way is to take the one risk, and get it away in the early morning, after straightening everything up, so that they'd never guess anyone's been there."

"You mean brick it all up again?"

"We shall have all night. It might mean that they wouldn't spot what we'd done at all. And, at the worst, if we were seen loading it up, we might make a good bolt, and get here safely enough. But we won't try for a taxi. There'll be less risk in a pick-up car."

"And which of us is to do the picking up?"

"You'll have to do that. It won't do for me to be seen round there. Or anywhere else for that matter. That was the kind of thing I meant when I said we've got to have our plans clear."

Mr. Brice was not given to demonstrations of feeling, but Mr. Flipp was aware that his remarks were not kindly received. However, all the reply he got was a quiet: "Perhaps you'd better tell me what the plans are."

"There's only one thing possible with the mess I'm in. They'll find out that I'm not at home within forty-eight hours, and they'll be scouring the whole country. I've got to get my travelling done before that.

"I'll help you get the stuff here, and I'll wait, if you can't do better, till three o'clock in the afternoon, but I shall want my share in cash before then, so that I can clear, and so that I shan't need to get in touch with you again."

"You know that's impossible."

"I don't know anything of the kind. I know it's got to be done. And, anyway, how can you say it's impossible without knowing what will be there? There may be jewels—it's most likely there are—and there may even be cash in some form.

"I shan't be unreasonable as to the amount, and I'll take jewellery or anything portable for the larger part, if that's what's there. But in any case I shall want two thousand pounds in cash. Bank notes—*clean* bank notes—will do. Of course, if the Goffe Collection is all or most of what's there, it'll have to be all in cash, and I shall want a lot more than two thousand pounds. But we'll talk of that when we see what there is.

"Only it will be best for both of us that I have a good sum in cash when I get away, and that I lose no time in the start.

"Best for *both*?" Mr. Brice's tone as he asked this was that of a man who was not offended or alarmed, but genuinely puzzled as to what it might mean.

"Yes. Best for both. I shall take some catching if I get away where I intend—I'm not trying anything silly, like going aboard a ship—and if I have plenty of money with me of the right kind. I mean that won't draw suspicion on to me when it's circulated. But if I do get caught I've only one thing left to do, and that is to come to terms with the police."

"Come to terms? How?"

"Yes. Make a deal with them to let me free if I tell them all I know about Coldwater's affairs. You can see whether it would suit you for me to do that."

"You would do that? I thought the lowest thieving scum in Whitechapel—"

"I dare say. But I'm not that sort. I'm not a professional criminal. I'm a respectable man, that's got in a mess through my employer's death. A man with a family to consider. You wouldn't expect, if there were no other way, that I should keep quiet about Coldwater's affairs because it wouldn't suit you for me to talk?"

Charlie Brice heard this, and made no reply. Mr. Flipp did not guess that, till his last hour, he would never be nearer death than he then was. The man who confronted him was far too cautious to commit violent murder except at a last extremity. But he was far too ruthless to hesitate if his judgment should tell him that it would be the safer course.

He considered that a body might lie for an indefinite period unsuspected in that untenanted flat, and that Theophilus Flipp was the only man who could know that he had ever entered its doors. But he remembered also that these were the rooms in which the booty was to be hidden, the quest for which had brought them together. Had he known of that empty house, the keys of which were in Mr. Flipp's hip-pocket, it is probable that the little weapon in his own would have been discharging its contents across the room within the next ten seconds.

But he did not know. On the other hand, he remembered that the job they had on hand for that night would be hard enough for two to accomplish, and might be impossible for one alone. He must have Flipp's help, even on his own terms. When—if ever—they should have got back with the booty here, he would consider how far it might be wise to talk in another tone. And, beyond that, he had more confidence in himself than his companion for such an enterprise as taking possession of a parked car. He knew that, in manner and address, he was far less likely to attract the suspicion of a passing constable. And, if trouble should arise, he was far more likely to be able to get out of it successfully than a man who was already bailed on charges of fraud. He was of unblemished character. He even had a proper licence for the weapon he carried, obtained through reports of attempted breakings-in at the laboratories. He was not in the habit of doing illegal things!

Beyond that, he might find some excuse, some reason, for being on the shop premises—even for having keys. He did not think Jessica would prosecute him for being there! Flipp's position would be more difficult. It would be far better for himself that he should succeed than that Flipp should fail.

Giving no sign either of these thoughts or the resentful anger that they subdued, he said "Well, we won't quarrel. If we find we shall need a car, I expect you're right that I'm the better one for picking it up. And we'll see what we can do about getting you off when we've found what's there.

"After all, it was your idea at the first, and I'll forgive you anything now except finding an empty hole."

"We shan't do that," Mr. Flipp said confidently.

Their minds went back to the time when F. C. Halters & Co. had been run by a man who had been no more than Coldwater's tool. At that time, it had been his favourite clearing-house for the stolen property that passed through his hands. But when the man died, Coldwater had told Flipp that he must have the business sold, and cease to use those premises. In any case, he did not believe in occupying any such lair for too long a time.

But he had talked to Charlie Brice in a different way. It was a place he had given up—yes. But it was one he might use again, if they could find some woman to buy the business who would become an unconscious dupe, or a willing tool.

Then there had been the fact that he had concealed from Flipp, who had most of his criminal confidences, that he was resorting there again; his anger when Flipp had discovered the fact; and his recent disuse of other old resorts.

Thinking these things over, Flipp had approached Charlie Brice, because he had seen that his hold on Jessica would give him the necessary access to the premises, and that they might easily accomplish together that which would be perilous, if not impossible, for himself alone. The pooling of their knowledge had made that appear certain which had previously been no more than a precarious guess. And finally there had been that flash of inspiration by which Flipp had guessed the hiding place itself, and recalled the occasion when Coldwater must have made his cache.

After that, it had seemed no more than a common prudence to wait till the marriage with Jessica, so chivalrously proposed, so plausibly hastened, should give her husband a legal right to explore the premises, and take quiet possession of what might be concealed thereon.

Even when the unforeseen disclosures of Sneaky Dawes started the police investigations, it had seemed prudent to wait from day to day, so long as they had been confined to that part of the premises which Henry Coldwater had recently occupied.

But with the marriage deferred, if not broken off, and the skinning of Coldwater House suggesting what might happen to Jessica's back-room if the police should turn their attention again to those premises, as they would be likely at any moment to do, it was clear that no more time must be lost, if the illicit fortune were not to evade the hands of those whose wits had been first to penetrate where it must be.

"We'd better walk," Mr. Flipp proposed, as the time for starting approached; "it's a goodish way, but we're more likely to be seen on the Underground. And you'd better go ten minutes before me. If you find anyone there, you can say you've come to see Mrs. Lee. Considering that she was to have married you this morning, you ought to get away with that, even if it is a bit late to find her still at the shop. I've got both keys here—the smaller one's for Mrs. Lee's door, on the right hand at the top of the passage. The other lets you in to the outer end of the part Coldwater used to have. You won't need that. You can pass from one to the other when you're inside. But I don't see why we shall have to go in there at all, unless it's to get those tools that you say the police left. I'll come up after, and, if everything's all right, you'll have the door two or three inches open."

Mr. Brice made no objection to this. There was evident reason for him to be the one to make sure that the premises had been closed for the night, and he had had no intention of walking through the streets of London by the side of Theophilus Flipp.

CHAPTER XXXII.

An Entrance During the Night

MR. FLIPP, walking unobtrusively up the Edgware Road, and avoiding to look at anyone he encountered—for he knew there is no surer way of drawing the attention and holding the memory of others than to look directly at them—asked himself if he were not a fool, and was unsure of the right reply.

He saw that the high water marks of danger would be the moments when he should enter and leave the Pritchett Street passage, and he could have avoided those risks entirely had he been willing to trust Charlie Brice to recover the hidden booty, and to render an accurate account. But that was what he was sure that he would not do. He would be far more likely to say that he had found nothing at all. He had reluctantly given his confidence to a man whom he did not trust, when he had seen that he was likely to have an easy access to the room, such as he himself could not hope to get. He would never have done that had he thought the engagement to be insecure. It had become inevitable that the treasure should be shared. Worse, with the prosecution threatening, it had become inevitable that his own share should be restricted to what it would be possible for—and he could persuade—Brice to find in immediate cash. But to let him go alone might be to sacrifice not part, but all that his wit had come so nearly to gain.

Besides, there was the practical difficulty that it was likely to be a two-man job. But for that, and the equally important fact that he had ready a place to which the findings could be removed, it was certain that Brice would have got to work without informing him of what he did.

And whatever fears Mr. Flipp might have, his reason told him that the risk was not great. The police had, for the time at least, finished their search of those premises. They had gone elsewhere. Was it likely that they would keep a close watch, night and day, at the entrances of premises that had ceased to interest them? Why should they?

It would have been different, even, had he been going to the front of the shop, where there must have been a half-minute when he, or Brice, would have been under the gaze of neighbours or pass-ers-by as they unpadlocked the door. But it would be the act of a second to turn into the Pritchett Street passage. He passed it once, because there was a woman close behind him, who might have ob-served his entrance. The second time he was more fortunate.

Certain that he had not been observed, he went on to find a door standing ajar in signal that all was well. He entered, closed and locked it, and joined Charlie Brice, who had already taken off his coat, turned up his cuffs, fetched some tools from the further room, cut off the electric (heating) current, and commenced the removal of the radiator in Jessica's sitting-room. Theophilus Flipp felt the first half of the battle was won.

He would have been less easy in mind, though it might not have been sufficiently ominous to change his plans, had he known that Mr. Jellipot had telephoned to Jessica that morning, and, on learning that the marriage had been indefinitely deferred, said a few further words which had resulted in her subsequently taking Millie Rapp— to whom it had, in any event, been necessary to give some explana-tion of her appearance at the shop at a time when she was supposed to be occupied in a more amatory manner—into a partial confi-dence; after which the two girls had engaged in a hard, dirty, and utterly fruitless probing of the loose boards of the shop floor, and the taking down of shelves to no better purpose than the disclosure of a small cupboard, which proved, after one moment of breathless expectation, to contain an empty ink-bottle and a tattered copy of the poems of Oliver Goldsmith.

Had the two midnight visitors looked into the shop, they would have seen evidences of the day's search in a counter that was piled with stock, shelves stacked against the wall which would be less easy to put up than they had been to remove, and linoleum that lay loosely upon the floor.

But, knowing their objective, they wasted no time on inspection of other parts of the premises. The old chimney had not been left, or superficially blinded, when the electric radiator had been installed before it. It had been bricked up in a solid manner, and then papered over with the rest of the room, as though to protest the finality with which the era of coal was closed.

Now they must break this brickwork down, with care to avoid what, at any moment, might be found to be concealed within, and without making a degree of noise which might penetrate to those who dwelt in the flats above.

So they worked, amicably enough, with no more than an occasional muttered curse for the pain of a grazed finger, or the noise of a slipping brick, happily unaware that, as midnight came, Mr. Jellipot, who had not retired at his usual hour, was rung up by Chief Inspector Combridge, to hear him say: "Well, I'll hand it to you! We've got the two birds in the bag. I'm speaking from the other side of Pritchett Street. My men saw them both go in an hour ago, about ten minutes apart. They'll be clever if they get out again, either back or front, without feeling something cold on their wrists."

"What are you going to do now?"

"Oh, just wait! They'll save us a lot of trouble if they know where the swag is, as I've no doubt you were right when you said they do."

"I didn't quite say that. I said it was a just possible thing."

"Well, it's more than that now. But we'll give them rope. It's burglary any time, but it'll be just as well for them to make it plain why they were there. I suppose you wouldn't like to come, and be in at the death?"

"No. I don't think I should. But I'm in no hurry to go to bed. You might give me another ring if there should be anything interesting to tell."

"Yes. I owe you that."

Inspector Combridge rang off, and Mr. Jellipot asked himself why he did not feel more pleased than he was.

He had some reason for satisfaction. His talk with Scotland Yard during the afternoon would almost certainly lead to the recovery of stolen property of substantial value, and the ultimate conviction of two particularly dangerous criminals. If his guess were right, the recovered property would include the Goffe Collection, which would be a particular gratification to a most valuable client, who was also his friend.

And as to the girl—well, he admitted that he would have liked to see her pick up the reward. But he had done what he could. He had given her the first chance through the day. He could not have omitted to inform the police, and have suggested to her that she should watch her premises alone through the hours of darkness, against the entrance of two—or perhaps more—unscrupulous and potentially violent criminals.

He did not agree entirely with the views which Sir Reginald expressed with such picturesque vigour. It seemed to him that the arrest of criminals might be as important for the peace of the community as the recovery of stolen property. But, have it as you would, he saw that there should be satisfaction for all in the drama which proceeded in Pritchett Street, even as he sat thinking here, to its natural end. If he felt restless and ill at ease, he must consider the deletion of that solitary after-dinner cigar, which he would be most reluctant to lose. The telephone rang again, and he saw with a start, as he took it up, that he had sat musing until 2:00 A.M.

He heard the expected voice, and said: "I suppose you've made the arrests? I hope you've got something more valuable than those two."

"No. We haven't got anything nor arrested anyone yet. I've just rung up to let you know that we shall be putting the handcuffs on one more than you thought we should. Ten minutes ago, Miss Jessica Lee walked into the shop."

Mr. Jellipot was not usually short of words, but for a moment he had no answer to make. Then he said: "You mean she's joined the two men? What criminality is there in that, even if there is not some quite different explanation from what you suppose?"

"It means she's in with the gang, which I've always been half inclined to think. But it was rather clever putting off the marriage, as though she took the warning from you. They seem to have taken warning another way."

Mr. Jellipot did not discuss that construction of the event, which had a plausible sound. He said: "I think I'll come. I ought to do it by taxi in forty minutes, with the streets clear. I suppose you're not doing anything immediately?"

"No. We're content to wait. The party may not be complete yet!"

"Well, I'll come along. What's the address? Number 30, next to the fishmonger. Paddington 0626. Yes. I've got that."

Mr. Jellipot laid the telephone down. He rang up the nearest garage. He put on his boots. He wrote a note to his house-keeper, whom he was reluctant to disturb at that hour. He walked restlessly up and down. Surely the taxi should be here now! But the clock showed that scarcely four minutes had gone since Inspector Combridge had rung off.

He picked up the receiver again. "Paddington 0626. That you, Inspector? I've been thinking. I'm sure I shouldn't wait longer if I were you. I think I should raid the place. You don't know what may be going on inside."

"That's our difficulty. We don't. We don't know where we are now. It isn't burglary, if Miss Lee invited them there. We might be made to look fools, unless we can catch them actually going off with the swag. Even then they'll say, more likely than not, they were heading straight for us, to pick up the reward. No, I don't think I can raid them yet."

Mr. Jellipot heard finality in the Inspector's voice, and recognised the reality of his dilemma. He also heard the bell telling him that the taxi was at the door. He said: "Well, I'm coming now. If you'll take my advice you won't wait till I arrive. But if you can't raid them, I can."

Could he, if the police should obstruct his way? It was a legal point on which he would have time to reflect as he travelled rapidly northward through the quietness of the deserted streets. Having considered it, he hoped, for more reasons than one, that the question would not arise.

CHAPTER XXXIII.

SOMETHING MR. JELLIPOT DID NOT FORESEE

JESSICA had gone to bed almost immediately when she got home, and to sleep almost as soon, for she was exhausted by excitement and physical exertion which she was not in good condition to stand. She slept for two hours or perhaps three, and found herself suddenly wide awake from a vivid dream of the kind which will leave the mind disquieted even beyond what would occur had it been a real experience.

Wandering in the realm of dreams, her mind had discovered with a sudden clarity that which it had not been sufficiently alert to observe in the waking day: the significance of Charlie's anxiety that she should throw out the electric radiator from the living-room at the shop and reopen the grate. It was to be one of the first—the very first—things they were to have done during the week which he preferred that they should spend there, rather than at Bexhill, as first proposed. And he had said that he would superintend it himself!

She did not think thus in the dream, of which all she could recall was a cascade of descending bricks, and Charlie with a bricklayer's trowel in his hand, about a yard long, and a face of devilish exultation, such as she had never seen or imagined that he could have. But before that there had been some threat, some terror, at which her heart still beat madly, though she could not recall what it had been.

But she had waked with the conviction—the *certainty*—that she knew where the treasure lay, and the reward—the reward for the Goffe Collection alone—was to be sixteen thousand pounds!

Sixteen thousand pounds. It might have been sixty thousand, or as many millions to her, and it would have been no more. It was limitless wealth. What can be greater than that? And Mr. Jellipot had given her the hint, and the time, and she had wasted it pulling down shelves in the shop! When she might have thought—have *known*.

There was the sting. The reward had been hers to take, and her own denseness had let it go.

Was it gone yet? With a sudden hope, she supposed not. But with reflection the hope shrank. Morning might bring the police again. Mr. Jellipot had hinted plainly that her time would not be long. They might be there now. More likely, if she had the courage—which she would not have. If only Bob were in the next room! He would have come with her. He was someone on which she could have relied. But for those hateful police. Perhaps not illogically, the thought hardened her mind so that, for the first time, she seriously considered getting up and going to investigate during the night. The police had robbed her of Bob, who would have been both loyal and obedient to her. She would take from them the triumph of disclosing the hidden spoil!

She hesitated again, doubting whether her single strength would be equal to breaking through the barrier of bricks. But, in the morning, who should she employ? Could the man whose actual hands laid the treasure bare claim priority in the reward? She was too ignorant to answer that. But she saw that her chance was now. It was a development that Mr. Jellipot had not foreseen. He neither claimed to foretell the fact nor interpret the meaning of dreams.

She hesitated again as she dressed with nervous, trembling hands, thinking of the corning child whom it was her first duty to guard. Suppose she should overstrain herself at the unfamiliar toil, and some harm should come? But the thought had a double edge. It was for the child that she would win the security that wealth can give—and which is needed most by one who can take no pride in a father's name. She must be careful in all she did.

She let herself out silently, watchful at first not to disturb Mrs. Renshaw, who had appeared uninterested in what she had told her when she came home, seeming to be able to think of nothing but Bob during recent days; and then going slowly, step by step, down the creaking stairs. But being out in the cool night air, she walked briskly through empty streets.

A policeman crossed with long strides from the farther side of Bayswater Road, and surveyed her curiously. "Out a bit late?" he asked with a kindly and yet penetrating curiosity in his tone.

"I'm going back to the shop. I believe I left the back door unlocked."

"Far from here?"

"No. Not far. About ten minutes' walk."

He paused a moment, his eyes still surveying her dubiously. Girls of her age alone in the streets at 1:30 A.M. were usually in need either of the protection or the detention of the police. He saw much at a glance, as it was his business to do. Her figure. The wedding-ring on her hand. The look of strain that might be caused by fear that she had left a shop door unlocked, or, more likely, by more urgent troubles.

But he saw that she asked no protection from him, and she appeared to be doing no wrong. He had seen enough of her to identify her beyond doubt, if there should be later need. He changed his cloak to his other shoulder, as he said: "You can't be too careful about shop doors these days. Good night."

She went on with somewhat greater confidence than before. She had been, as it were, permitted, by those who watched in the night. And, although they had taken Bob, it gave a feeling of safety to think that there were policemen who moved in the darkness, vigilant for the protection of such as she.

But when she came to Pritchett Street she saw no policeman, friendly or not. The street appeared to be deserted from end to end, as far as the dim light allowed her to see. It was certainly silent of any tread.

She had determined to go in by the back way, which would be more sheltered from observation. Like Mr. Brice, she had recalled that heap of tools which the police had left so neatly stacked in the outer end of the partitioned room that had been occupied by Henry Coldwater a few weeks before. Knowing her way about more familiarly than he, she went directly to that door, intending to select the most useful tools and then make her way to the room she sought through the inner passage.

She moved quietly, though she did not doubt that she was alone. She switched on the light, and saw at once that the tools had been disturbed. On a closer inspection, it was evident that some were not there.

With greater caution, and a heart now beating quickly, she approached her own room. She heard movements, and low voices, one of which she knew, if not both.

So far, those who were within, more concerned to maintain a difficult silence themselves than listen for outer sounds, had heard nothing of her.

For a long minute she stood there debating silently what she should do. She could retire, admitting defeat, and leave them to remove what they should find. She would not do that. She could walk boldly in with the good right of one who was on premises which she leased, and demand that they should come to terms which would be satisfactory to her. She might—she probably would—have done this

173

but for the deterrent memory of Charlie's face as it had appeared to her in the dream. There was no sense in that, for it had been no more than a fantasy of her own mind, for which he should not be condemned, but feeling is not sense, and it held her back.

Finally, she could retreat unheard and call the police. But this she was reluctant to do. She hesitated, even now, to betray the man whose kisses, however falsely they had been given, however coldly received, she had accepted till yesterday, to an amount of trouble as to which she could no more be sure than she yet was as to his degree of treachery towards herself.

Seeing no tolerable course to take, she stood rooted in doubt, and as she did so Mr. Flipp straightened a weary back.

It had been amazing to find how thoroughly Henry Coldwater had done that walling-up. Yet there was ultimate hope to be seen in the thickness of bricks, for it was surely more than any bricklayer would have considered necessary simply to close away a chimney no longer required.

Now they were near the moment of triumph or defeat. There was little more to demolish, but they were impeded by the debris of the work they had done. Mr. Flipp, still rubbing his back, said: "It's those shovels we're wanting now."

"Well," was the reply from the man who was on his knees struggling to pull one of the last bricks away, "you can fetch them, can't you?"

Mr. Flipp cast a considering eye upon the state of the arched hole. He had no mind to be absent when the moment of discovery should arrive. But he saw that there would be no danger of that.

CHAPTER XXXIV.

A BULLET FOR MR. FLIPP

CHIEF INSPECTOR COMBRIDGE considered Mr. Jellipot's remarks, which had done nothing to improve a position he did not like. He knew that, if anything were happening inside those well-watched premises which required his interference, he would be blamed for inaction if he delayed. He knew equally well that if he should blunder by challenging those who were acting within their lawful rights, and in so doing warn them against the completion of what would have proved to be either crime in itself or evidence of earlier guilt, he would be equally blamed. It was one of those positions in which it would be of no avail to say that he had acted with wisdom or official propriety. He had to make the right guess; and if he could do that, it mattered nothing whether his reasons were wise or foolish, his actions regular or the reverse.

He supposed Mr. Jellipot's suggestion that he should raid the premises immediately to imply a doubt of whether Miss Lee were in friendly understanding with the two men, and he saw that if she were not, if she had surprised them in a burglarious entry of the premises, her position must be unpleasant and might be acutely dangerous. But was that a reasonable supposition?

Was it not more likely that she had joined them by appointment for a common object? And, if so, what justification was there for his interference at all? If they should have discovered Henry Cold-water's secret hoard, and be caught in the act of surreptitiously moving in during the night, it might be hard to explain. But unless or until they should be observed in such an attempt, the answer was that he had no right of interference at all. That might not have deterred him, at least from an enquiry as to what was going on, which, in itself, would be natural and proper procedure, but for the fact that such an intimation of police watchfulness would almost certainly prevent the demonstration of criminality in which he hoped to catch them. By his impatience he would have defeated his own end.

The position was rendered more unsatisfactory by the fact that the back of the premises was not under close observation. There was no opportunity of judging, by lights or noises, what might be happening within. He spent ten abortive minutes in walking round to the front, and ascertained no more than that all was dark and quiet there, and that his men were alert for any exit that might be attempted from the shop door.

Being impatient of inaction, and considering that Mr. Jellipot would soon be on the spot, and that he would much prefer to make his decision independently of further advice, he compromised with his doubts by going with Detective-Sergeant Twinkler very quietly up the passage, to give a nearer inspection to the back rooms, where he had no doubt that the three were.

At this time a moon had risen, to add its contribution to the diffused light of the city streets. It enabled him to find his way up the passage without difficulty. He approached the window of Jessica's living-room, in which he could see that there was a light, though the curtains were closely drawn. Low muffled noises came from within. Listening intently, he heard voices, though he could tell nothing of what was said. Very cautiously, he examined the window. If he could have raised that, though by no more than an inch—

Twinkler touched his sleeve. He pointed to the nearby door which opened into the narrow hall that divided the rooms. The upper half of this door was glazed. Dimly visible, a woman's figure could be seen standing outside the door of the lighted room, and obviously listening to that which went on within.

Inspector Combridge had no difficulty in recognising Jessica, and he saw all that that position implied. It exonerated her to an extent for which she had cause to be thankful at a later hour.

As he looked in, she saw him, and the sergeant's burlier form at his side. But she took no notice, was indeed barely conscious of them, for she had just heard the suggestion that Mr. Flipp should fetch the shovels, and his step approaching the door.

The door into the room which had been Henry Coldwater's was immediately opposite. It stood open, as she had left it when she came through. Fortunately, she had switched off the light. She had just time to step across the passage and move behind it before Flipp appeared. The dim moonlight was paled by the stream of light that came through his opened door, and fell in a shaped pattern almost at Jessica's feet.

Either from caution, or because he felt no need of more light than he already had, he did not touch the electric switch as he entered the room. He went on to the shovels, found them without difficulty, and came back with one in each hand.

Jessica stood, afraid to move, scarcely concealed from him at all by the half-opened door. Facing her now, and with eyes adjusted to the meagre light, he saw her distinctly, and guessed correctly who she must be.

It was evidence of the nimbleness of his wits that he gave no sign. He must consider what was best to be done. He was uncertain to what extremity his companion might go. As they worked, with their coats thrown aside, he had had opportunity to notice the shape of that which Mr. Brice's hip-pocket held, and it had not been a welcome sight.

He had heard that even habitual burglars think it imprudent to carry arms. He had remembered that when two people are engaged in an unlawful occupation, and one commits a murder, both are liable to be hanged. He had hoped earnestly that there would be no trouble with the police that night.

Now he had five seconds of reflection, of doubt as to how or whether he must tell Brice what he had seen, and fearful speculations as to what might follow, and then Jessica went forever out of his mind, for he saw the two who watched in the yard. They had drawn a few steps back while he had been picking up the shovels, but the moonlit yard was lighter than where he stood, and he had a reputation for seeing well in the dark.

Still giving no sign that he saw, he went back to the lighted room. Charles Brice heard him coming, and drew his head and shoulders out of the hole they had made. His face and clothes were smeared with brick dust and mortar. There was blood on a grazed cheek. He spoke on a high-pitched note, his self-control shaken for a moment by the excitement of the event. "It's there," he said. "All the lot! Give me one of them."

Mr. Flipp's voice had an excitement of another kind: "There are two cops in the yard."

"Sure?"

"They're just outside the window now."

Mr. Brice stood motionless. He had no mind to admit defeat. If he had lost that which was hidden two yards away, he might still claim the rewards. Plans, excuses, explanations, raced through his mind, in all of which Theophilus Flipp figured as the greatest difficulty which must be removed, or explained away.

Mr. Flipp observed an indecision he did not approve. He spoke again: "If they keep quiet, it means that they're sending someone round to the front, and they're waiting till they get there. We'd better try bolting that way. It's the only chance."

He looked at a man who gave no sign that he had heard, and his patience failed. With those other charges over his head, with the plans of flight that he had made, he had no intention of being caught there by the police if there were still a chance of getting away. "You can do what you like," he said, "but I'm off while the going's good."

He ran out into the passage. He could be heard stumbling in the dark shop. He fell sprawling over the linoleum that Jessica had pulled up, and not properly laid again. He could be heard fumbling with the bolts.

For the first moment, Charlie Brice stood still. He had no inclination either to follow or to interfere. Whatever tale must be told would be simpler if it did not require to be confirmed from another mouth. Flipp could do him no better service than to get away and be heard of never again.

But Mr. Flipp's dash for freedom had been observed by those who looked through the passage door. It became plain to Inspector Combridge that the time for action was forced upon him. He put a whistle to his mouth and blew a signal which was echoed a moment later from the farther street.

Charlie Brice waked to swift activity at the sound. It was evident that Flipp was not destined to get away, and if that were so he must be silenced by other means. He reached the shop as the last bolt was withdrawn, and the door opened.

"Hands up," he shouted, loud enough to be heard in the street, as in fact he was, for there were constables round the door. But he did not expect, nor did he intend to give opportunity to be obeyed. It was a case for a bullet through the head—through the *top* of the head—almost a miss, but not quite. He did not doubt that he was a good enough shot to do that.

The shot came as Flipp pulled the door open, and had his foot on the top step. He pitched forward, so that his body sprawled on the steps, with his head on the pavement below.

Mr. Brice came forward confidently to the little group of constables who were raising him up.

"He fell, didn't he?" he asked. "I suppose it frightened him when I fired. I only did it to stop him. I fired over his head."

In his shirt-sleeves, and smeared as he was with dust and blood, he presented a curious spectacle, but the voice with which he spoke was quiet and self-possessed. The constable who looked up from the fallen man answered respectfully: "I'm afraid it's worse than that, sir. I'm afraid the bullet didn't go high enough. I should say he's in a bad way."

Mr. Brice had no doubt he was.

CHAPTER XXXV.

REWARDS FOR JESSICA

JESSICA acted on instinct rather than reasoning the consequence of what she did as she heard the sound of the police whistles, and saw Charlie Brice dash towards the shop, pulling the pistol out as he ran.

She saw Inspector Combridge at the door, and went forward quickly to let him in. He pushed past, with Sergeant Twinkler behind him, neither of them taking notice of her.

They ran into the shop, where Brice stood at the door with his back to them, the pistol still in his hand.

Inspector Combridge made a gesture towards him. "Handcuffs, Twinkler," he said briskly. Now that he knew that Jessica had not been a consenting party to that midnight entry, he had resolved to act with a high hand. His instinct told him that he controlled an event which went well.

Charlie Brice found himself seized from behind on both sides at once. He was too prudent to make more than verbal protests, though those were of some vigour as the handcuffs clicked on his wrists.

The constable had bent over the fallen man looked up in doubt of whether Combridge might not be making a mistake which he would regret.

"It was an accident, sir, I think. The gentleman meant to fire over his head. He was just bolting out of the shop."

"He'll have a chance to explain that, and a good deal more," the inspector answered grimly. He had seen enough to have a different opinion of what had occurred, though it might be wrong.

"I tell you," the handcuffed man went on, in a tone of one who endeavours to remain calm in the face of intolerable and stupid outrage, "I was here with Mrs. Lee's consent, and in another moment I should have found what you'll all be thankful to see. How the man had got in I don't know, but I should think anyone could—" His voice broke off as he caught sight of Jessica at the back of the shop.

Inspector Combridge noticed the startled glance, instantly though it was controlled. He said dryly "Well, here she is, to speak for herself. Do you mind telling me, Mrs. Lee, why you arranged for this gentleman to be here during the night?"

"I didn't know—I didn't arrange anything of the kind."

"So that's settled," the inspector remarked, with the good humour that comes easily in moments of success. But his prisoner made no answer. He saw that, till he had thought out what line of defence the position would still allow, there might be more wisdom in silence than further protests. And next moment Jessica had withdrawn. She might not be prepared to support the assertion that he had been there with her consent, but her feeling was still too confused willingly to bear damning witness against him, if she could avoid it by moving away.

Retreating thus, she came to the door of the living-room, and looked at the chaos of excavation within. Mr. Jellipot stood at her side. "I don't think," he said, "that there's much more to be done there. If I were you, I should go in, and pick up one of the shovels, and lock the door."

A few minutes later Inspector Combridge came through from the shop. The handcuffed man had been put into a taxi. A doctor and an ambulance had been found for the wounded one, who was not yet dead. Now he had leisure for a few words with Jessica, and to ascertain what had been happening in that lighted room.

He put a hand to the handle, which did not yield. Mr. Jellipot stood by.

"Who's inside there?"

Mr. Jellipot answered a question which may not have been addressed to him.

"Acting on legal advice," he said amicably, "my client, being busy, has locked the door."

"What's the game?"

"It appeared desirable to avoid ambiguity as to the actual discoverer of the Goffe Collection and other trifles that may be there."

"You mean they're all in that room?"

"I have hopes."

"Then you might be good enough to tell her to open the door."

"I don't think she will keep us long. And after all, you know, it's her own house."

"I know some other things besides that."

181

"You know," Mr. Jellipot suggested mildly, "if I must say something which I am reluctant to stress, but which should not be entirely forgotten—you know who suggested that you should be here tonight."

"I'm sorry, Mr. Jellipot. I shan't forget that in a hurry. But the fact is I ought to be back now. There'll be a question of how Brice is to be charged. And we can't make a mistake about that."

"You might charge him with damaging a particularly good chimney. That would be a safe start, and then murder and burglary and other trifles could be added from time to time at your own convenience. But if you want to get off, I think you might leave this to me, with the assistance of two or three of your brawnier constables, for the protection of property of unusual value."

CHAPTER XXXVI.

Some Matters That Might Be Worse

IT was four o'clock on Friday afternoon when Inspector Combridge called at Mr. Jellipot's office, and was received by the solicitor with a yawn which he made no effort to suppress.

"I should have gone home," he said, "before now, had I not been expecting you, and had something rather particular to communicate, for the fact is that I am not young enough for the kind of night which I have just spent."

"I don't suppose they do any of us any good," the inspector replied, from more experiences of the kind than Mr. Jellipot was ever likely to have, "but I'd risk worse than that for the haul we made."

"You feel that, on the whole, you have reason for some satisfaction?"

"You can put it higher than that. Even Sir Henry's been purring over me like a cat with a kitten she hadn't seen for a week. And the best of it is—and I dare say this'll be something you haven't heard. Flipp came round this morning—it seems that he isn't very seriously hurt, the bullet having gone a bit high, whether it was meant to or not, and just ploughed along the top of his skull—and he's been spitting it out against Brice for all he's worth. Coldwater had been using him—he's his nephew really—him and his firm's laboratories, without their knowledge of course, for melting down things that were too risky to trade as they were, and not valuable enough to put aside for a few years, as he did with that tiara we got last night. And he made use of him in other ways that won't bear as much daylight as they're likely to get.

"Flipp went on for an hour as fast as a quick shorthand writer could take it down. I expect it'll end in that crack along the top of his skull being about all the punishing that he'll get. But there's one thing that you'll be sorry to hear.

"He won't admit that he knows anything about the murder, nor has any idea who did it. He says it wasn't Brice, because he knows he was miles away at the time.

"I pressed him hard about that, because I know you think we've got the wrong man, and after what you've done for us, I should have liked to pay a bit back, but he seems genuine. Unless, of course, he did it himself, which he wouldn't be likely to say. I only gave up when the doctor asked me whether I thought he'd be more use to us dead or alive."

"It was good of you," Mr. Jellipot replied gratefully, "to look at it in that way; but it was about that matter I wanted to talk to you as well as a man who is half asleep can be expected to do. The fact is that I had a client here this morning who mentioned having killed Coldwater, and in view of the present prosecution we agreed that it would be best to have the facts put into the form of an affidavit, which I have here for you, properly sworn. I didn't think it would be wise to certify it myself, so it was sworn before Mr. Sturdee on the floor below."

Mr. Jellipot was searching among the papers on a piled desk, and drew out a heavy foolscap envelope, already sealed, and addressed to Chief Inspector Combridge, C.I.D., New Scotland Yard, S.W.1.

"You needn't open it now," Mr. Jellipot went on, "because, though it is a very clear statement, and easy to understand, it is also rather long, and before you reached the attestation I should in all probability be asleep, but if there is any point that you would like briefly explained I don't mind doing the best I can."

"I can't very well ask anything till I know who it is."

"It is Mrs. Renshaw, of course. I practically told you that when I said that it wasn't Bob."

"But she told me that she didn't know one end of a bayonet from the other!"

"She mentioned to me having said something of the kind. It seemed to be curiously on her conscience. As far as I could understand, it was because you believed her so simply. She said it felt like smacking a baby. But, as a matter of fact, she was on V.A.D. work in Serbia during the war, and got mixed up in the actual fighting as few nurses have ever done. I should say that, if she hadn't actually killed a man with one before, there can be few women who know more about how to push it in, and just what harm it would do."

"Well, it shows how appearances can lead one astray! I should have called her one of the nicest, quietest women—"

"As I have no doubt that she is. If I have said anything to give a contrary impression, it was unintentional, and I must withdraw it."

"Well, with this confession—"

"It is a word to which Mrs. Renshaw very strongly objected. She would describe it as a statement of fact, to which she has added her reasons for what she did. You see, although Jessica was not a blood relation, she felt a special responsibility, because she had given her dead husband a promise to guard her, in which she felt that she had failed rather badly."

"So she thought she could square things up by killing the man?"

"She did not act, as I understand, in reference to what had occurred, but to prevent that which might still be to come. She judged that while Henry Coldwater lived Jessica's honour and happiness were gone, and that even her life would not be safe, if he should suspect her of being in possession of any of his criminal secrets, when he found that it was a form of life she would not share.

"Even had he been willing to marry the girl, she would not have regarded it as a solution, but only making the position worse than it already was.

"When you read her statement you will see she says that she went, after all she already knew, with an open mind, but the man's own words—he appears to have been in a particularly vile temper after the beating that Mr. Forbes had given him, and he may have been further irritated by the moral precepts of Bob Longworthy, so, to that extent, you may say that those two gentlemen had some responsibility for the event which followed—decided her that there was only one way by which the girl's happiness and her pledge to her dead husband could be secured, and when she saw that particularly suitable weapon near to her hand, she felt that the occasion could not be improved."

"And yet she seemed to want the girl to marry this fellow Brice."

"Because he had deceived her as to his character; and she believed him to be genuinely attached to Jessica, and likely to make her a good husband. She says that she was anxious that the girl's future should be secured before she admitted what she had done."

"I suppose you don't know where she is now?"

"No. I didn't ask where she was going, and she might not have told me if I had. But she understood that I should let you have that document without delay, and the consequences that would naturally follow. Her chief anxiety appeared to be that Bob should be released promptly."

For the first time, as he heard this, a doubt entered Inspector Combridge's mind. "You don't think," he asked, "that she's faked this up to save the boy?"

"It is a possible theory, but it is one which I see no reason to favour."

"I expect you're right. Anyway, I won't keep you talking now."

Inspector Combridge was already at the door when it occurred to him that the most mysterious incident of the whole affair was still unexplained, and might make the innocence of Bob Longworthy still far from clear.

"Perhaps you'll just tell me," he said, "if Bob cleared off before Coldwater was killed, how he came to be washing the bayonet afterwards? Or, perhaps, he washed it first, to get it ready for his mother to use?"

"The explanation is simply that it wasn't Bob but his mother who went into the yard. Obviously, it was a thing that no man in his senses would do. But on Mrs. Renshaw's part I think it was rather shrewd. She saw Coldwater's hat and raincoat hanging on the wall, and the thought came to her that if she could show herself in that disguise she might get people to assume that it was a man's work. She told me that she went out into the yard holding the bayonet as conspicuously as possible, and washed it elaborately. She didn't venture to look up much, as she naturally didn't want her face to be seen, but she says she couldn't have believed that so many windows could seem so quiet and empty of life. She thought the ruse had failed.

"After that, she went back, hung up the hat and coat, put the bayonet in its place, and let herself out at the front door. She calculated reasonably that no one who happened to be looking out of a back window would be likely to be doing the same thing at the front three minutes afterwards, even if it had been from one of the houses that face the Square.

"The unfortunate thing was that though Mrs. Renshaw looks the taller when they are both normally dressed, she and Bob are about the same height, and there was a still more unfortunate similarity, particularly in colour, in Henry Coldwater's raincoat and bowler hat, and those which Longworthy wore at the parade."

"Well, I suppose we've got to the truth at last, and we can call it a full day."

Inspector Combridge departed, and Mr. Jellipot felt that the circumstances justified a taxi home, in which he slept well.

He was late in getting down to Basinghall Street next morning, and he had already read a newspaper announcement that Scotland

Yard was anxious for information concerning the whereabouts of Ursula Renshaw, who was wanted in connection with the Coldwater murder.

The sleepless energy of Inspector Combridge had supplied the Press with a full and adequate description of the missing woman, who, early yesterday afternoon, had taken out a car which she had garaged for some months, and had been traced to Andover, where she had stopped for tea, and for some minor mechanical adjustment of the car. The number and description of the vehicle followed, and with those particulars appearing in every daily newspaper, it did not seem probable that she would remain long at liberty, even apart from the inquisitions of the police.

Mr. Jellipot read with gravity. He had some sympathy for the hunted woman, but he saw that it had become a matter which must now be left to the orderly and relentless process of English law.

* * * * * * *

It was an hour later, as he was on the telephone discussing with Sir Reginald Crowe the apportionment of the reward which would give riches to Jessica Lee, that Richard entered and laid an early edition of the *Evening Standard* silently on his desk. He read, under emphatic first-page headlines, how a wrecked car had been seen, battered by swinging waves, at the foot of a Dorset cliff, and how P.C. Swithers, climbing perilously down, with a rope's support, had identified it as that in which Mrs. Renshaw had fled.

Mr. Jellipot read it twice. Well, it might be the better way! Better than the anxious strain of trial, the expectation of slow-coming death at the hangman's hands. But then he thought of those securities which his client had been careful to realise—and with such secrecy—before admitting what she had done. He thought also of the cool resourcefulness which had put the dead man's garments to such confusing use, and which, had she not found that the suspicion which missed herself fell on her son, would almost certainly have secured her from detection.

"I shouldn't wish to embarrass our friend Combridge with the opinion," he thought, "but I do not suppose it to be one of those cases where the body will float ashore."

187